AUNT JUNE

Aunt June

JENN DUNDEE

Jenn Dundee

For every person who has ever felt forgotten and left behind. You are not alone.

You matter.

Acknowledgements

I want to thank my husband, Chad for his unwavering support during this process. Saray, for her enthusiastic reviews and encouragement. And my mother, Carole for feeding my love of literature and raising me to believe I can accomplish anything I set my mind to.

Thank you all, for everything.

Chapter One

Looking desperately for my bus beyond the busy horizon of skyscrapers and accepting defeat to the power of time, I relaxed against the steel pole holding up my cover from the blaring sun. My skin dampening with every moment in the early summer heat, I stood uncomfortably close to a man who snored rather loudly on the bench.

The man was undoubtedly a drunk by the looks of the empty bottle clenched in his scarred and crusted left hand. Homeless men and women were far from uncommon in Detroit, I hoped wholeheartedly where I was headed would be different. It was common in my hometown, to see people living on corners and out of grocery carts. It never got easier to watch. To walk by, looking the other direction.

I began to recite the different lives he could have lived. Passed out on a bus stop bench, in the middle of the afternoon during this heatwave. As my mind wandered from my mundane daydreaming of a man that I knew nothing about, I caught a glimpse down the road of my bus as it took a wide turn around the corner headed to me. Looking back at the man

I pulled a few dollars out of my pocket and slipped them into the bag he had wrapped around his foot.

As I loaded onto the bus, with my duffle bag weighing down my left shoulder I pushed past the crowded sections, making my way back to an available seat in the walkway.

I took a seat, averting my eyes from the woman asleep on the floor in the last row. No matter who she was or how she got there, it was clear she needed the rest, and it was no place of mine to interfere and cause a stir.

I had a long trip ahead of me with no intention of resting while en route to the airport. I spent my whole life here; I didn't know anything other than the city. I was familiar with the bus routes, the people. I knew Detroit. I could find my way home from any corner of any neighborhood blindfolded the way my parents let me run wild. They never bothered me much with where I was, who I was with, where I was going. I had freedom.

We pulled to my stop in Romulus, I took a moment to look around as I walked to the entrance of the airport. This was the last time I would see this city for the next few years, assuming I'd make it back at all. Surprisingly to myself, I realized I didn't have much attachment to that place. I checked my bags and found my gate rather easily thinking back on what I was leaving behind.

My parents and I had a complicated relationship. Mom wasn't always aloof, passive, and angry. She used to play soccer with me at the park down the street every Saturday and take me for ice cream after. We did arts and crafts over winter while we spent time cuddling in the house safe from the cold. She taught me nearly everything I knew about art. Dad owned a financial consulting firm and worked out of town fairly often, but he was only away a few short days at a time. Mom and I would spend every moment together playing games and exploring the city together.

Around my ninth birthday is when things seemed to shift in our home. I still wasn't sure what it was that changed, I came home one day from school and neither Mom nor Dad was there. Dad was away for work, but my mom would never leave me home alone. I panicked wondering where she could be and ran next door to our elderly neighbor Camille, crying asking her if she had seen her. When she realized I was alone, she brought me inside and made me dinner while we waited for her to return. Things weren't the same after that.

Camille's apartment was filled with floral designs and expensive-looking artwork on her walls. It would have been impressive had it not been for the thick smoke-filled air illuminated by the sunlight she let stream through her lace curtains. She smelled of cheap cigarettes and even cheaper perfume, but she was kind to me. I think a lot of it was a pity, there was little chance she couldn't hear the way my parents fought through the echoing hallway. She watched over me when my parents couldn't.

Mom began staying so busy I hardly saw her, she was irritable and sad more times than not, so when she managed to be home with me, I tried my best to keep quiet and out of her way. She was different like a switch flipped and turned a light out in my life.

When Dad came home from his trips, he would bring Mom flowers and gifts. Take her on dates and spend every minute with her. This left little time for me, but I didn't mind, it was easier to be left alone. He tried relentlessly to make her happier for those several months, with minimal success.

Until one-night dad came home early and walked in to see me sitting on the couch watching TV and eating cereal. I was ten then, I knew how to use the stove but when Mom went away for the night, I had free reign to do anything I wanted. When Dad was home things were more structured, thankfully he hadn't walked in on me watching *The Shining*. It was my favorite, but I wasn't allowed to watch rated R movies. He would have lost it.

I was sent to bed moments after he got home, it was nearly midnight, well passed my suggested bedtime. The next thing I knew it was three in the morning, Mom was home and fighting with Dad in the kitchen. I put a pillow over my head, trying to muffle the sound. Dad's trips became more consistent and lengthier after that night.

The arguments were relentless for a while, every weekend Dad was home to visit was spent walking on eggshells. I always questioned why they stayed married in the first place. They were happy once and lost it somewhere along the way.

From what I understood my mom visited Michigan from her home in Washington to protest a pipeline with her sister June who was arrested at the event. When Mom went to pick her up from the jailhouse, she ran into my dad while he was there delivering paperwork. He was hired by the city to establish financing for that same pipeline. She knocked him and his papers to the ground in the heat of the moment, while frantically yelling at a security guard about letting June out. They used to laugh about it, how the first thing Mom ever said to him was a threat to his life to some extent. He said he fell in love instantly with her fire and passion.

It took Mom a while to come around, of course, being that they met on opposing sides of the event that day. They never confirmed or denied anything, but from what I gathered she caved to his advances a short time after plans for the pipeline were denied for improper funding. I always enjoyed thinking that was his grand gesture of goodwill to my mother, tanking the financing for the project because he knew how much it meant to the woman, he hardly knew but was madly in love with.

She agreed to one date because she and June were meant to board their plane and head home that next evening, but Mom was swept off her feet and never made it to the airport. June was upset with her when she got the news they were engaged, said it made my mom a traitor of everything they stood for. It took some time, but Aunt June came around to their marriage a short while after I was born. I believe her visit when I was younger was the first time my mom had seen her since the protest years before.

Chapter Two

Mulling over the ideas in my head of what would become of my life, and of me by daylight tomorrow, I boarded the plane, got comfortable in my window seat, and drifted off to sleep. It had been an emotionally and physically exhausting few weeks.

I was staying at my friend Cameron's, while my parents were attending a fundraising gala on the night of the accident. Cameron's mother, Mrs. Morris, came walking into her son's room requesting my company downstairs. The look in her eyes burnt into my mind. I can recall the ringing in my ears and extraordinarily little of what she said to me. The police were there, my parents had been in an accident.

I walked downstairs with movements that didn't feel like my own and I couldn't tell if I was still breathing as the officers explained to me what happened. My dad was driving, lost control of the car, and went off the road. Mom wasn't wearing her seatbelt and died on impact. My dad never made it to the hospital. He came too long enough to tell the responders where to find me that night, then just like that, he was gone.

I've replayed that scene in my mind hundreds of

thousands of times, every dream I had turned nightmare. Every car I walked past started a chain reaction in me always resulting in a panic. Wondering if the passengers knew the dangers they were facing. Wondering if my parents knew what was happening as they went over the rails. I walk myself through the scenario of each car I came across meeting their same fate. Off the freeway, or onto the sidewalk. Flying into oncoming traffic.

My parents have argued in the car before, Mom's been known to push Dad while he drove. Thinking how likely it was my mom pushed him or grabbed the steering wheel. Again. This time she just went too far.

To know more than the police about what likely really happened only seemed to make me feel worse.

The days that immediately followed my parents' death are still a blur, Mrs. Morris insisted I stayed with them until her and my parent's attorneys decided what to do with me.

Four days ago, I was drowning in a sea of black hats, dresses, and suits. There were crowds of people hugging, introducing themselves to one another and providing their condolences. It seemed for a while there as if their sympathies were more for their own benefit than mine, but I decided it didn't matter either way. I stood there, at the front pew, a foot from my parents' lifeless bodies laid so sharply in their sturdy cherrywood caskets, accepting the world as it came at me. I remember so little about that day and yet every detail was etched into my mind.

I had enough pity built from complete strangers in one day than most people would experience in a lifetime. I didn't need pity. I needed out.

Out of Mrs. Morris' house, out of the city, out of my own mind. Cameron seemed to be the only one who understood. If he ever caught me in long stints of silence, he didn't question me, didn't try to get me to talk about anything. He would just sit with me, staying by my side while leaving me alone.

As I walked into Mrs. Morris' kitchen that night, she cut me a piece of a condolence casserole and set the plate on the table anticipating my taking a seat. She explained the phone call she received from my mother's sister, June. I would be leaving at the end of the school year to live with her in Colorado. Mrs. Morris seemed more worried about how I would take the news of Colorado than she did about me moving there. Being so far away from everything I knew.

I had been excused from my classes indefinitely, despite that finals were beginning for the end of the year. My teachers allowed me to take my final exams at home and to turn them in by end of the week. Which left me in the house with Mrs. Morris all day. She was a kind woman, we got along fine on a regular day to day basis, but these were not regular days.

Cameron brought all six of my exams home Monday and I had them turned in by Wednesday morning. Regardless of my interest in wanting to concentrate on something other than what was happening, I couldn't carry the thought of sitting through hour-long classes full of people who knew about the unfortunate turn my life had taken. Followed of course, by classmates who would never speak to me otherwise, apologizing as if they knew me, or as if they cared.

Chapter Three

I had met June once before when I was about six years old. She came to Michigan to see my parents and was almost impossible to forget. Even being so young and never seeing her again after those short few days, I thought back on her time with us often. She liked to play with me and my trains for what felt like hours and in every room she walked through the smell of Palo Santo seemed to follow her and lingered long after.

I could hear her late at night crying from the kitchen after I had been sent to bed for the night while her and my parents talked. I never found out what happened her last night there. When I asked, Mom simply told me that her sister was an emotional person who lived and expressed life differently than the people I was accustom to. I didn't entirely understand what she had meant but I guess it wasn't worth understanding because June left, and I never heard from her again. I'd concluded not all that long ago that she was probably just one of the many family members who came requesting loans of sorts, and when turned down sentenced themselves to exile.

How ironic that she was destined to be my new guardian.

Growing up I had spent a lot of time wandering the city, with my dad out of town so often and Mom constantly busy with her own life I had more free time than I knew what to do with. At thirteen, most of my evenings and weekends were devoted to the Detroit Institute of Arts walking each hall, reading every plaque. It was my home away from home.

It gave me time to think. I've always preferred to be in my own company so being alone was never a real issue, but there were spurts of loneliness in life that seemed to dull when I was surrounded by the collections. I felt like the answers to all my questions were hidden in the artwork on the walls or somewhere in the displays.

I anticipated seeing a new Edgar Degas exhibit the weekend before my sixteenth birthday, but that was put on hold. My dad took me to meet his colleagues instead, he always spoke about my working for him after graduation and I usually went along with any plans he made. I figured there would be time later to explain to him how little interest I had in running a financial consulting firm. That day made it seem so real, I knew I needed to tell him sooner rather than later. Knowing how upset it would make him, I decided to wait until my birthday had passed so as to not ruin it for myself at the very least.

The proper time never seemed to arise, so I kept it

to myself, biding my time. I always thought there was time.

It was nearly midnight in Aspen when we landed. I made my way to the luggage carousel and gathered my bags, scanning the area in hopes I would recognize my Aunt. A decade passed since I had seen her last and any pictures I saw growing up were dated for long before I was born. I wasn't sure who I was looking for but was too embarrassed to ask over the phone the evening before.

A soft, almost inaudible voice came from directly behind me, "Kenny, is that you?" Turning around I was toe to toe with the most vibrant woman I had ever seen. She yelped, in what seemed like excitement and immediately threw her arms around my neck slamming my bags, and almost myself to the floor. I recognized her scent, from so many years ago. Palo Santo. I had found my Aunt June, even more brilliant than I remembered.

She released me from her embrace and quickly grabbed my face between her gentle calloused hands while never releasing her gaze from mine. It felt as if she was staring into my soul and made me feel secure in the most uncomfortable manner.

Her look softened and seemed misplaced in time for a moment. She gathered herself as quickly as she seemingly lost herself and smiled again, welcoming me home.

June grabbed one of my fallen bags off the floor and threw it over her shoulder, almost knocking herself to the ground. Walking through the parking lot I was grateful I didn't leave my jacket in my luggage, the air was cool, damp and smelled strongly of wet pine needles. The night was quiet, almost eerie aside from a few passing taxis loading and unloading a handful of travelers.

Even in the dead of night, with only streetlights to illuminate the parking lot Aunt June reflected the light from the stars, she had so many colors and jewels and gems decorating herself I wondered if we needed the streetlights at all. She was speaking so quickly about her excitement to have me there it seemed taking a breath may have been the death of her. Her jewelry ringing as she put my belongings in the trunk of her Nova, the bumper was rusted, and the paint was faded but it was clear she took great pride in it.

Aunt June opened my door and ushered me into the front seat, staring again for a few moments, smiling, as she shut the door. Scurrying around the front of her car to the driver's side door, her dark green cloak caught in the bumper almost yanking her to the ground. She laughed at herself as she regained her balance and motioned to me that she was alright. Not missing a beat, she yanked her cloak free and continued to the driver's seat.

"It is so wonderful to see you my sweet Kenny, it has been so many years, and look at you, so grown and strong. How old are you now? You must be at least twenty." Shooting me a quick wink she went on again in her ramblings.

"You are going to love it in Carbondale. Of course, where we are going is no 'Big City' but has its perks and I hope you manage to feel right at home. If there is ever anything, I can do for you to make you feel more comfortable just say the word. I was thinking maybe tomorrow we could go into town for lunch. It is such a beautiful town best known for its Springs, you must join me in the Springs some time, you would absolutely love it. I would spend eternity there if I could."

Aunt June chatted about her town for the next twenty or thirty minutes about how wonderful it was. The stories getting more excitable as we passed the Carbondale Welcome sign.

As we passed through town, every building I could manage to make out of the darkness appeared to be closed and after only a few stop signs along the route, the buildings and houses grew further apart.

Being well after midnight I suppose it made sense. I'd heard that small towns shut down early, but I always assumed that type of lifestyle was more novelty than reality. Back home in Detroit after my parents were asleep for the night I would stand on the edge of our balcony and overlook the city below, the noise and bustle never-ending as if sleep were futile.

The roads got longer, and the turns sharper as the houses off the road became obsolete. It felt as if we had been driving for hours, between my dead phone and the broken clock on the dash, there was no way to know for sure.

Just ahead, on a small hill I saw a massive plot of land, accompanied by a humble sized home. The lights were all on, including the strings of lights spread out between the trees, and patio. We slowed at the end of the drive and turned in, there were open windows that undoubtedly never closed, a large, sculpted patio, trees and plants that engulfed the home entirely. It was immaculate.

"Home sweet home, welcome." Aunt June gleamed at me from behind the steering wheel urging me to look out the window. I noticed a small waterfall at the end of the drive, brought to life by the string lights and full moon. As we got out of the car, five large mutts came running to greet us. They jumped in excitement and June didn't seem to mind a bit, she appeared to almost encourage it, despite the mud they left all over her cloak.

I always wanted a dog of my own growing up but my parents were set against it. They didn't believe dogs provided any real benefit to a home, only more stress. I just assumed they were right, and from this encounter alone, I don't argue it. She introduced them to me as my cousins, which only made the situation more uncomfortable. As I found no way to word the discomfort and confusion it caused me, I chose to let it go.

Walking through the back door with my bags I stopped dead in my tracks, amazed at everything I saw. There were nearly no walls, everything was so open, covered in tapestries, photos, collectibles, charms, life-size sculptures, and art surely of which came from all over the world. Aunt June crept up behind me as the dogs' barking subdued.

"Don't mind the mess, I would lie and say I hadn't gotten around to cleaning, but truthfully my home looks like this pretty much all the time. I feel the mind and soul work best when constantly surrounded by the things you love. Come with me I'll show you the rest of the house." Aunt June reached for my hand with a loving motherly smile. "You can go ahead and just leave your bags there if you'd like, we can grab them in the morning." My mother always hated clutter and my things left lying around. I once left my backpack in the foyer and she grounded me for a week.

The dogs were outside, two of them sitting patiently by the door to be let in and the other three cuddled on the patio furniture soaking up the cool night breeze. Their content eased my mind, I reluctantly went along with placing my bags on the ground where I stood and took a deep breath as I stepped away from them, giving my hand to Aunt June.

Passing through the kitchen she allowed my hand to drop and continued forward with her tour as I stood stuck for a moment. From the ceiling to the scratched hardwood floors was a lattice window overlooking the open land for what surely stretched a mile, though impossible to see in the dead of night. Catching up with Aunt June in the living room, all around me were paintings, large crystals placed delicately on the floor along the wall, one barely noticeable behind the ghost chair gently swaying from the ceiling. There were three large open windows that extended from the floor to the ceiling, with ferns overgrowing on either side. The exposure to the outside world was unnerving.

A cat tree opposite the windows towering over her housed a disheveled feline Aunt June gently pressed her nose against. "This is Bongo, he came in the house one night and just sort of never left. So, I made him his own little castle." Looking up at me, still one hand on Bongo she looked proud of her accidental friend.

"Your room is upstairs in the loft, of course you can redecorate it however you see fit. I left it mostly empty so you would have room to grow into it." Aunt June lead me up the stairs from the living room and into the loft. It was nearly closed off, except it didn't have a door.

At that moment it dawned on me there wasn't a door insight since we walked in the back, surely, I had to be confused from the exhaustion. My new room was significantly smaller than the one I had with my parents, honestly if I didn't know better, I would say my room back home was larger than June's house. There was a twin-sized bed in the back corner, with a blue quilt and what looked to be the most comfortable pillow I had ever seen. The walls were white and empty, aside from a charcoal mural across from the bed.

I glanced around for a clock, with no luck. Simply a lamp on the nightstand and an incense stand, accompanied by a tiny Buddha on the dresser.

Aunt June suggested I get some rest and excused herself. After plugging my dead cellphone into the charger beside the bed I found myself face down in my pillow, a light scent of lavender deep within it carried my mind off into a deep sleep.

Chapter Four

The sun leaking through the window beside my bed woke me that next morning, along with the sound of dogs running through the house below. I rolled over and turned my phone on, I had several missed calls from Cameron; calls immediately followed by text messages.

The time on my screen read four in the afternoon. I slept through the day entirely. Sitting up in bed still adjusting from the extraneous trip, I took the time to review the mural on the wall across from me. It looked like something out of a Banksy exhibit I saw back home the year before, only the medium wasn't right. The center focused on charcoal lines creating a vast image of a woman emerging from flowers, which engulfed the length of the wall. Only a handful of flowers were doused in red spray paint dripping to the floor, which seemed to give it a quiet life. It was all together a very tastefully done project.

Walking downstairs the sound of wind chimes swaying outside the open windows echoed through the house. Aunt June was in the kitchen, sitting at a pinewood table centered in front of a lattice cased window, sipping from a bone china teacup, and reading what appeared to be a local paper. I searched the cupboards for a water cup. Aunt June peered up at me and inquired about how I was feeling as I filled my glass, watching the hummingbirds float around the trees outside.

People were asking how I was feeling relentlessly as of late, but not one of them seemed as if they really wanted to know. It sounded tirelessly robotic, like they knew that's how you approach someone who recently experienced a loss, not in a manner that would imply they were genuinely concerned to hear about my thoughts and feelings. I was angry, I was angry at everything and everyone. I was hurt, my heart stopped that night in Mrs. Morris' Livingroom and hasn't started back. I felt empty, alone and forgotten. As if the world had just left behind everything I was as a person. Everything my parents were, seemingly no longer mattered.

I've felt anger and resentment towards everyone who would have the audacity to promise they would pray for me. Insisting my parents were in a better place now and that they were watching over me. I didn't believe a word of it.

I'm angry June. I'm angry and I'm upset. I'm completely alone and I'm lost. That's how I'm doing.

"I'm okay. Still tired from the trip, your bed is very comfortable." Of course, she wasn't ready to hear how I was. I don't even want to hear me say it out loud. So long as I keep quiet and just move forward, I can keep the numb I've grown close to, still clinging to my chest, just a little longer. I can live with that feeling. The second I talk about it; it will become real. And I'm not ready for that either. "I'm sorry I slept so late. I don't usually do that."

She gave me a knowing glance as if she could hear my thoughts. The look in her eyes was almost unnerving. She looked at me for what felt like an eternity before looking back at her tea and taking a sip. "It's been a long week. I'm surprised you managed out of bed at all. You should get as much rest as you're able, you've got nowhere you need to be, no tasks that need doing as of yet. Enjoy it. Take this time to take care of yourself. Come on over here, take a seat." She pulled the chair next to her out from under the table and motioned for my company.

"Actually if you wouldn't mind, I could really use a shower right about now. The flight was pretty rough, and I think it's been a few days." It had been a difficult twenty-four hours, and a hot shower was long overdue.

Aunt June stood from her chair. "Of course, I'm so sorry, the bathroom is right down this way." I followed her to the other side of the house and into the bathroom. No door. So there is a theme. As confident of a young man I may have been, showering and using the restroom in a bathroom with no door may just be the line I'd have to draw.

As she pulled a towel and washcloth from the closet, I took the chance to inquire, considering she still didn't seem to think anything about mentioning it herself. "Aunt June, is there any reason you have no doors?"

She looked at me with a slightly cocked and confused gaze that instantly straightened when the concept took hold. "Oh, my dear I have been living alone for so long I never thought much for how that might affect other people." She broke into a short yet infectious laugh. "I began studying Feng Shui years ago and learned of the negative impact too many doors in a home can cause. So, I just decided to be done with them all. Took them all out and never thought about it again. Along with some plants and properly placed furniture, this place has been much calmer. Now there are the curtains, tucked to the side here, just be sure to pin them back to the side when you're done." She smiled encouragingly and grabbed my shoulder as if we were bonding over the topic.

Aware of my discomfort over the situation she promised to look into the best way to respect my privacy while still respecting her *Chi*. I couldn't help but roll my eyes after she excused herself from the bathroom to allow me the little bit of privacy I may be entitled to here.

After I was sure she was back to the kitchen and far enough away, I turned the shower on, testing the warmth with caution. Once the temperature was acceptable, I found myself in the predicament of getting undressed. What if she forgot to tell me something and came back in. The best resolve I could conjure was to get undressed in the shower. Removing my shirt and jeans quickly and throwing my towel over the curtain rod, I stepped into the tub still wearing my boxer shorts, removing those only once certain I was alone and fully hidden behind the shower curtain.

There were small glass bottles on the built-in shelves, and several bars of soap on the corner carousel, nothing was labeled. One was purple with what looked like flowers crushed inside of it, another was a dark green that hadn't been used as far as I could tell. I took to a smell test, the green bar smelled of sandalwood and seemed my best bet. I figured the glass bottles must have been some type of shampoo or bubble bath, they either smelled like nothing or like flowers. I opted for scentless.

At last, I could put an end to the most awkward shower I ever had. After getting dressed and ready for the evening I asked June what everything was in the tub. She laughed and walked me through it, having not purchased a hygienic product in twenty years she makes the shampoos herself. The bars of soap, which I learned are also shampoos, she buys from a friend of hers from down the street who makes her own products. She explained her disinterest in commercial beauty products due to their extensive use of chemicals.

Her way of living gave me hesitation, she was a little obsessive, but overall her home-made products smelled better than most store-bought products.

Also, I couldn't recall a time in my life I didn't need lotion after a shower before, whereas at this moment, my skin felt just fine. Not that I intended to express that.

It was about time for dinner and Aunt June suggested we go into town to eat. She said there was a wonderful Mexican restaurant that she visits regularly for their margaritas. It was like watching a kid on Christmas the way she excitedly grabbed her bag and frantically searched for her keys before we left.

Chapter Five

On our way into town we passed several boutique shops that looked to be closing down for the night, a bar that looked to be opening for the night and what had to be the entire Carbondale population out and about on walks with their dogs and kids. I was used to busy, but this was a different type of busy. Nothing was loud, no one seemed to be in any hurry to get anywhere, everyone seemed...*happy.*

The restaurant needed a renovation, the outside looked rough, especially in comparison to the ones surrounding it. It seemed the historical red brick look was big in this town, but this restaurant was left out of the loop with its wooden siding cracked and corroded. Even so, the moment we stepped inside I was in awe. The windows were opaque, allowing in minimal light from the gleaming sun outside, the whole restaurant decorated with bright reds, greens, yellows, and blues, everywhere you looked there were candles and patio lights strung from the ceiling. It was no wonder Aunt June enjoyed this place so much.

Over dinner, June spent most of our time asking about my life in Detroit and about her sister over the years. It was difficult to talk about her, talking about her made me miss her more. I tried to muster up information for June as best I could but surrendered to my predisposition when my eyes began to swell. June placed a gentle hand on my forearm and changed the topic to focus more on myself. I was embarrassed, to sit at a public table and choke up speaking to a woman I knew so little about. I took the cue and straightened out my back recalling some of the things I enjoyed in my spare time.

I explained my interest in art, and the Detroit Institute I spent so much time at. I went on about my school, the way the uniform would chaff, and how the teachers would demand so much from each of my classes. The only class I thoroughly enjoyed was Art History. I took a swing at art classes in and out of school, Aunt June looked so proud, grinning brightly. I told her about one city showcase where a mixed-media piece of mine was selected to show through a course outside of school my Freshman year. That was a big moment for me, I remember getting the flyer from my instructor and how proud he looked of me. I enjoyed him as a whole, he was very worldly, knew too little about too much and was always hungry to know more. He took every bit of information he ever learned and applied it to his art in some manner or another.

I let my story of that evening fade out in recollection of the events that followed, leading to the night of the showcase. I arrived home that night, the house empty, my parents away at another charity event I'd supposed. I put the flyer on the counter next to the coffee machine expecting my mom to see it in the morning and headed to my room for the night. There was another week until the event, I was in no rush to see if they would manage to fit it into their schedule.

The note disappeared the next day, so I assumed Mom got the message, but when the showcase came and went with no word from her, I decided she must not have. If I had seen her much that week I would have asked.

The night of the Showcase I took the bus back home and reflected on the evening. There were a few people who had stopped and inquired on the piece which to this day still baffles me, but the real surprise was that someone bought it. The gallery called me the next morning and said they had taken an offer for it. They said they would have a check for me with my share by the end of the week. It was a proud moment and in a weird way almost made up for my parents not making it. My teacher had given me a photocopy of the piece before we sent it for the show, so I put the copy up in my room, received a check for fifty dollars in the mail from the gallery and it was never mentioned again.

The remainder of our dinner was spent with small talk pleasantries and June sharing some stories of her travels over the years. Which brought us to the end of the meal and a conversation I was unprepared for.

Aunt June looked defeated as she closed her

eyes and drew a deep breath into her chest. "Kenny. We don't have to talk about anything you're not ready to talk about. But I want you to know, I loved your mother. And I am so sorry I wasn't there for you all these years, especially the funeral."

My jaw clenched tightly, and my body went rigid as she spoke.

"I should have been there. Your mother was a beautiful woman with a kind heart, but we both allowed our pride the best of us. I should never have stayed away. When the accident happened, I ... " Aunt June's voice began to crack and her eyes blurred red with tears. "I wasn't here. And I am so sorry. I should have been here. I should have been there. I was halfway across the world trying to make my life worth something, unable to recognize what I had here all along." She reached for my hand across the table, my body still frozen I was unable to reciprocate. "I just want you to know that I'm here now." Her hand placing gently back in her lap. "I am here now. And as long as I have control, I'm not going anywhere."

It was clear to me she loved my mother. I had no doubt in my mind. Growing up when mom would tell stories about her childhood, she always fondly remembered June. Until she didn't. One day the stories stopped all together. I wanted to reassure June that it didn't matter to me, that I wasn't angry with her for not being there. She wouldn't have made a difference, but I didn't have the heart to share that with her. It seemed crass. I congregated a smile and gently shook my head, hoping she would understand I didn't hold it against her. She seemed to accept my gesture as she wiped her eyes delicately and let out a small scoff at herself.

"I'm sorry. I didn't mean to make this night about all that." She waved her hand in the air as if to wipe away the last several minutes from our lives. "What do you say we head out of here and get back home?" That same loving smile fought its way to me past her swollen cheeks as she signaled to our waitress for the check.

The ride home was quiet, her A.M. radio playing jazz softly at a hushed volume. June pulled into the drive and we were greeted by the welcome crew of dogs. She put her arm in mine as we walked to the house, swaying with every step. My mom used to walk with me the same way, it was eerie how alike they were with absolutely nothing in common.

Chapter Six

The next day waking with the sun, the smell of cedar and clean linens filled the air. I made my way downstairs to see June, on her head, knees on her elbows and feet in the air completely upside down in the middle of the living room.

"Ah, Good morning!" She rang out in a singsong voice bringing her feet to the ground before her and stood to face me, beaming. "Are you ready to hit the road? There are a couple of errands in town I was hoping to run, and maybe you would be willing to take me?" She grabbed the keys off the hook by the back door and began jingling them in front of her while giving me an encouraging glance.

She wanted me to drive.

I had driven before, a few times here and there. But any care I had to be in a car, much less driving one, was far gone. My dad took me to get my permit several months before, shortly after my sixteenth birthday. We drove around for a few hours a week or when he made it back in town, it was nice to spend time alone with him away from the stillness of our home.

Most of my peers would be thrilled, but I couldn't

bring myself to do it. She took my rejection very well and asked no questions which was a relief. I wasn't sure at the time how I would answer her if she did.

We pulled onto Main St in town and headed for the post office. The gentleman behind the counter seemed to know June well, it was almost sweet watching them chat like schoolyard friends. Looking through the window I could see an actor's theater across the way and promised myself to stop in and check it out when I got the opportunity. June seemed she would be a while and I was curious what else was nearby, so I took the initiative to wait for her outside. Noticing a couple of restaurants and a pool, I figured if I was ever much of an outdoor activity type of person, I might have been relieved to see that. There was a sense of easement, however, to see there were options and I hadn't seen the rest of town yet.

June stumbled out of the post office, hidden behind a large rectangular cardboard box, I quickly went to the rescue as it came slipping out of her hands, seconds before it hit the ground. June shouted in a panic followed by immediate relief when she noticed the help. "Thank you." Her eyes closed for a moment. I offered to carry it to the car, and she raced over to the trunk, popped it open and lead the box safely onto a dark green moving blanket.

After securing the trunk, we drove down Main to a shop with massive glass windows. A sign out front read The House, looking around inside it appeared to be an event space that could be rented out but was currently housing local art for sale. I noticed most of the work displayed was professional-grade, it was incredible. I was accustomed to seeing fine art at the Detroit Institute, but seeing such incredibly crafted pieces from small-town locals was refreshing. June was gleefully welcomed by the young girl behind the counter and called me over, breaking my entrancement and bringing me back to reality.

I made my way to the counter and was immediately mortified.

"Taylor! This is my nephew Kenny, he just got here a few days ago from Detroit and is going to be starting school here in the fall, I think your parents mentioned you would be starting your junior year as well, so I figured while we were in town we would come by and give you two a chance to meet." Aunt June looked so proud of herself. As if she had just pulled one over on everyone. I could feel my face getting hot and my eyes starting to burn. *I've been here two days and she's trying to set me up.* I mustered out my pleasantries but could feel myself calm slightly as Taylor giggled and shook my hand.

"It's great to meet you Kenny, your Aunt speaks very highly of you. Says you two share a talent in the arts?" Taylor smiled warmly and I felt a moment of gratitude for June. Even if she had certain intentions with introducing me to a seemly attractive girl my own age, it didn't mean we had to be any more than friends. And I was in no position to pass on friends. June went on asking Taylor questions about an event she was expected to be in early the next year. She gave June a manilla envelope and said it was full of all the information she would need and waved us both off as we left. Taylor seemed like a sweet girl, maybe school wouldn't be so awful after all.

Once June and I were alone in the car, she began passing me fluttery eyes and nudging me as we drove away. I let her have her win, she went on about how popular Taylor was with the volleyball team at school and how she was part of the National Honors Society.

While I had no interest in meeting a love interest, it certainly wasn't the worst to have someone I knew for my first day at a new high school. Especially someone June seemed to know so well; it gave me a sense of comfort.

Our last trip of the day was to get a television for my room. I was grateful she offered the night before, and I wasn't put in an awkward position of pretending I didn't mind not having one. I missed watching my slasher films the last few days and was grateful the chance was coming soon. We headed straight home from there and I was ready to binge-watch the DVDs I had packed in my suitcase.

Chapter Seven

We pulled up the driveway and popped the trunk, once we got the box from the post office out, it was a matter of where to take it. I was almost sent flying over my own feet when June took her end of the box and started heading to the other end of the patio, away from the house.

"Where are we taking this thing?" I peered over her shoulder and saw a shed, with flowers around its perimeter and two tiny windows with shutters, one on either side of the door.

Aunt June smiled with excitement "I've been wanting to show you this since you got here, but I knew you had some big adjustments to handle. So, I decided to give you a few days first." As she worked the door open without dropping her end of the package, I saw a shadowed hoard of items inside, we maneuvered in the dark for a moment as she guided my way to set the box on its side in the center of the room. She threw her arms in a big ta-da "This, is my studio!"

As she flipped the lights on, I took inventory of the shed. It was spacious, though it didn't look like much from the outside, there was a loft area, stacked with clear tubs all overflowing with ribbons, paint, trinkets and wood. Nothing seemed to make sense together, but it didn't to make sense standing alone either. There was a manual pottery wheel, electric Kiln, easels, paintbrushes the size of sewer rats and much more.

I stared baffled for a moment taking it all in. It was incredible and only made sense considering her line of work. I knew she was paid for her art, though I didn't realize the extent.

"This is where the magic happens. My best sellers are my pots and vases, but the real treats are the canvas work. I keep this place full of anything and everything I could need to create my pieces. Which is where this bad boy comes in handy." She placed her hand lovingly on the mystery package we lugged in from the car. "I haven't been able to do much canvas work in a few weeks since I've run out of the material. It usually takes just over a month to come in, I think you're my good luck charm." She opened the box and requested my help in removing the contents. It was a massively rolled unstretched canvas. I helped her move it to an open space on the floor under a corner table.

Heading out to the house Aunt June locked the shed door diligently and handed me the key. "This is your copy. Everything in there is free to use at any time. I'm a firm believer that art is an expression of self when the world seems to be caving in on you. It keeps a person guided moving forward in life. Without it we are nothing." She closed my hand, the key in my palm and ushered me towards the house. "I'm thinking it's time for some late lunch, maybe a little kale and quinoa. And tonight, grilled veggies and chicken, what do you think?"

Food sounded wonderful. It had already been an exhausting day, though all my days seemed exhausting by then. All I wanted was food and a good movie marathon to fall asleep to at this point. Realizing we left my television in the car, I put the studio key in my pocket and let June know I would be in after getting it from the backseat. June had lunch ready and brought mine to the loft just as I got everything set up in my room. She asked what I was going to watch first, and I slid her my favorite movie from my bag I still hadn't unpacked, *The Shining*.

I figured it would be a stretch, she had a Zen way of living and horror films may not suit her well. But I invited her to watch it with me. To my surprise, she accepted the invitation with excitement. She grabbed her food from downstairs as I put the movie in, and we sat on the floor. She was watching my favorite movie for the first time and it seemed strange to me that being her age she never came across it before.

Though she wasn't the best film companion, she asked questions the whole time, it didn't stop either of us from enjoying our time together. My parents would never watch it with me, whether it be because they didn't have the time, or they just didn't care to.

When the film ended, I asked what kept her from watching it over the years, it was apparent she didn't have a weak stomach. In a laissez-faire manner, she explained that she had spent most of her life on the road. It was easier not having a television to cart around or to spend time or money at the theater because every moment of her life was dedicated to being out and exploring. It seemed reasonable enough, she had a certain wanderlust about her.

She went on as she collected our dishes from the floor. "When I settled down here years ago, I finally invested, then I went through that Chi phase and my consultant threw them right out the window. I tried to be a good student for as long as I could, but I couldn't do it. I have a television in my room now, though I can't say I make much time for it, I do love my soap operas." I involuntarily laughed; it may have been the first time in a month. It felt strange but for that moment hearing her talk I felt weightless. There were so many things about her I didn't know, and so much more about her world I wasn't sure I would ever understand.

Aunt June said she would be in the studio out back if I wanted to join her or if I needed her for anything, so I took advantage of the time to rest. I put in another DVD and was asleep before the main menu loaded.

Chapter Eight

I woke up a while later with momentarily no knowledge of where I was but could hear Otis Redding through a speaker downstairs, and a hint of raw onion wafted through the air. I had been asleep for hours and June was making dinner. I offered to help before she left my room earlier that afternoon, to which she clamored with excitement. I missed cooking, back home it was a relaxing pass time for me, and I was ready to get back to it. But it appeared my window for today had come and passed.

She was singing along off-key as I walked into the kitchen apologizing for being late, she lowered the volume on her dial turn radio that sat on the counter insisting it was no trouble. She was almost done, and simply glad she wouldn't be eating alone.

I looked around the kitchen for something to pass the few minutes before dinner was ready. June had already set the table and didn't leave me much to do. On the right end of the living room, there was an eight-foot-long forest green curtain pulled from one wall to the other reaching floor to ceiling, I noticed it my first morning here but hadn't made strides on my curiosity. I figured it must have been a makeshift door, as the bathroom had, closing off the only room I hadn't made my way into yet. Aunt Junes.

Leaving June to reference her cookbook, I slipped across the living room. Curiosity finally getting the best of me. I pulled the curtain back and turned the light switch on to find a tidy, open space bedroom. Plants were hanging in the corners in macramé holders by a king-size bed, with an oversized down comforter and at least a dozen full-size pillows. There was adjustable lighting throughout the room and a yoga mat set up in the far-left corner, but what caught my eye was the artwork hanging directly above Aunt June's bed. A mixed-media canvas, signed by me.

Aunt June came up behind me so quietly she startled me. I immediately began apologizing, I had no business being in her bedroom without her permission. But she wouldn't have it, she insisted it was my home and I was allowed anywhere at any time.

She looked adoringly at the picture hanging above her bed.

"It's a fine piece of work Kenny."

I could feel myself turning red. My parents weren't exactly supportive of my art, it wasn't considered a serious career, so neither of them had much interest in the matter. "How did you get that?" Realizing how rude that must have sounded I tried to backtrack. "I mean, how did you know I had art out for sale?"

Aunt June shrugged her shoulders with a

smile and turned back towards the kitchen. "I didn't. I buy work from all over the world, when I see a piece I like, I buy it. It just so happens that this particular piece was done by someone I knew." Her tone gave way there was more to the story, but I didn't need her to tell me what I already knew. She was still checking in on me after all these years, she had been watching from afar.

The weeks went on leading to my first day at school, I had spent a lot of my time in the studio and chatting on the phone with Cameron back in Detroit. I still hadn't made friends in Carbondale, but I figured in time with school I would meet people my age and surely there was someone I could get along with. At least long enough to get me through the rest of high school. The plan was to graduate here and head straight back home to work with my dad's company. The condo was paid off thankfully, so it would remain under the trust until I was of age to take its responsibility on as my own.

Chapter Nine

Junior year started rather rough, the schools set up was different from mine back home, the classes were fewer but longer. The lockers were inconveniently placed in their own corridor rather than along the walls between classrooms. But with such a small campus it didn't seem much of a problem.

I didn't feel terribly welcome. All the students seemed to know who I was, who my Aunt was, and why I was there before the first bell. It was a very uneasy feeling. I could hear the other students making comments about my parents as I walked by, the rumor mills spinning in full force. The worst of them all was the story I killed my parents for their money and was taken in by June as a social experiment to see if she could *cleanse the demons out of me.* It was clear she and I were the town outcasts.

I spent the first two weeks at Carbondale High with my head down and my thoughts to myself. I ran into Taylor a few times in the hall and when I waved in passing, she turned away from me so quickly I wasn't sure she had seen me at all. Until on my final attempt to approach her, she whispered to who

I assume was her boyfriend, followed immediately by them both staring back at me laughing under their breath. It became clear I was the butt of her joke and wasn't welcome in her corner. Despite the false sense of inclusion, she gave me earlier that summer when we first met at The House in town.

While disheartening to feel so unwelcome in town, I had to remind myself every morning on my way to school I would only be here temporarily. My seventeenth birthday was coming up in early September and from there I had one more year. Then I'll graduate and would never have to see my classmates again.

June would ask me every evening after school for details of my day, I would lie to her just enough to make her happy. Her believing things were going so well, that I had made friends and my classes were interesting was all that mattered. She was a kind woman, and very involved in the community, I didn't want to risk her having any problems with any parents here or even worse, risk her trying to convince her friends to make their kids be nice to me. It didn't work so well with Taylor and I had no desire to give that another try.

Chapter Ten

A few days before my birthday, June suggested I invite some of my friends to the house for a bonfire and pizza to celebrate. I still hadn't come clean about my exact situation in school, but I wasn't lying as blatantly at that point. There were two kids in my third-period science class that were nice to me over that last week or so.

The three of us were partnered by the teacher to work together leading to our midterm. Samuel and Katie had been friends for years, neither of them seemed to really hang out with anyone at the school aside from each other yet everyone seemed to know them and like them. Katie planned on attending Arizona State University after graduation to study psychology and Samuel planned on playing football for the University of Alabama. Samuel was certainly the athletic type, tall and heavyset, highly energetic, I thought he would do well in college football. Katie seemed as if she would do well in the psychology field too, she was patient and had a certainty in herself that made me feel at ease and confident around her.

The day had come when June planned

on me having friends over, yet I still hadn't asked my group partners if they'd be interested in spending their Friday night with me. While they were exceedingly friendly and accepting of me, I had to remember they were partnered with me by force, not sheer willingness. As third period ended that day, I swallowed what was left of my pride and approached Samuel and Katie while they got their bags together for their next classes.

They were discussing a party Taylor was having that night when I approached them, which made my stomach even heavier.

Katie stared at me in confusion while Samuel gave me that great giant grin of his. "What's up man? Thank you for all your help with this project. It's nice to feel like I might actually pass something for once." Samuel shot Katie a sideways glance and winked "Katie here does her best, but I'm getting tired of carrying her weight." Katie laughed as she swatted his arm.

"Seriously Kenny, thank you, it was nice not to have to carry *him and his fat head* all by myself for once." Katie was still laughing as Samuel playfully rolled his eyes.

They had to be dating. They seemed so in sync with one another it was almost unnerving to be around.

It's now or never. The week was over, and I promised June I would deliver friends, so the worst they can say is they already promised Taylor they would be at her place. "I'm happy to help guys, science has never been my strongest area. It feels good to have some help myself." The bell had run to dismiss our class, and the tardy bell was soon to follow. "Well, I was actually wondering, I overheard you guys talking about Taylors tonight on my way over, so it's no worries if you can't, but I was wondering if you might want to come by tonight. Maybe some pizza and I was thinking about having a little bonfire too, if you guys were interested?"

Katie and Samuel looked at each other from the corner of their eyes for a moment. I was humiliated. I could feel my face getting hot and my hands were starting to sweat, there was no way they would pass up Taylors place tonight, I've heard the stories. When her parents go out of town her home turns into a night club, people were still talking about the party she threw over the summer.

Katie smiled and nodded her head "We'd love to actually. Samuel here was thinking tonight might finally be his chance with Taylor if he shows, but of the multiple parties he's tried to get lucky at, literally zero have worked. And I think it's become unhealthy, so a little change-up could do us both some good."

That cleared up my dating theory. Samuel shoved Katie on her shoulder pretending to be much angrier than he clearly was about her selling him out. I couldn't help but laugh at their playful banter, Cameron was my closest friend and we didn't seem to know each other as well as they did.

"What times this shindig happening?" Samuel started walking out of the door and down the hall, Katie and I in tow.

I suggested seven o'clock, and they agreed. Katie waved me off as she walked into her next class. Samuel appeared to be done with the conversation as he waved on to a few of his friends across the hall when the bell rang and he walked into the classroom across from Katies. I was in such shock they both agreed I hadn't realized I was on the wrong side of campus; I was now the only student in the hall, late for my final class of the day.

I was stared at and taunted as I took my seat, but I could hardly notice any of it. I just made plans with the only people in this school who have spoken to me since I started almost two months ago, and they agreed to come to my house tonight and celebrate my birthday with me. Only they didn't know that's what they were coming over for. But that wasn't important now. What's important was that they show. I wasn't sure I could handle Aunt June's disappointment if no one came.

After school I took off straight home, my stomach felt upside down and my throat was tight. *What if they didn't come? What if they agreed to come as a joke? What would Aunt June have to say about my lying to her about having friends?*

As I walked up the driveway the feeling of nervousness dissipated and was immediately replaced with sheer horror.

Aunt June had balloons, streamers and decorative plastic table cloths across the patio. All color-themed green and white. My bags hit the ground as she stepped outside with paper plates and napkins in her hand, also to theme. "There's the birthday boy! Ah, I am so excited about tonight, celebrating my Sweet Kenny's Seventeenth Birthday." Holding the green napkins and paper plates to her chest, Aunt June twirled around going on about how it seemed it was just yesterday she got the news I was born. She was clearly having a go at my expense, and thoroughly enjoying herself.

I couldn't bring myself to admit my distaste for the decorations. I hadn't even mentioned to Samuel or Katie that it was my birthday and even if I had, streamers and balloons were for children. I smiled at her and picked my bag off the ground as I started to make my way into the house, only for her to drop the plates and napkins on the table, stopping me in the doorway.

"Before you go in, I got you a birthday present." Grinning ear to ear with her hands clasped eagerly in front of her, she put her arm in mine and guided me to the bathroom, where a large plastic blue tarp was draped over the entranceway.

After momentarily soaking up the confusion she mistook for anticipation, she released my arm and baited me to rip the tarp down off the wall. I began to laugh, between the strangeness of June and the odd gift presentation, I couldn't help but find the situation humorous. I stepped forward and decided to have some fun of my own, pretending the tarp was one of her art pieces.

I started walking the length of the tarp, caressing my jaw with one hand, while the other stayed tucked across my chest. "You know, Aunt June I have to say, you have really outdone yourself, I've always wanted a tarp of my own. No sense in pulling down, I think it really ties the room together."

She rolled her eyes and tossed her hands in the air. "Fine!" She laughed, yanking the tarp from the wall.

"Ta-Da!" Aunt Junes sing-song voice directed my attention to the doorway, the curtain that would pose as a separation from the bathroom, and the elements of the rest of the house was missing, and in its place was a barn door, slid open exposing the bathroom in its entirety. "I know I promised months ago I would find a way to make this situation more comfortable for you, and I'm sorry it took me so long. I just couldn't bring myself to have a door in here again, I've grown to enjoy the openness too much. But you are a young man whose only request all this time was for a little privacy and I felt it was the absolute least I could do. So I made some calls, talked to some folks at the hardware store and I had them install it this morning."

I inspected the door, opening it and closing it as if living there for several months somehow erased the last sixteen years of using them regularly. I couldn't find the words to thank her enough so I opted for a hug, which was uncomfortable but seemed to be the only way I could express my gratitude properly. She had gone through an awful lot of trouble to do something that wouldn't prove any use to anyone but myself. It was the most thoughtful thing she could have done. Her only request was to leave it propped open any time I was not occupying the bathroom. That seemed a more than fair trade for my chance at some privacy in the house.

With only a couple of hours before Kaite and Samuel arrived, Aunt June requested the RSVP for the evening so she could order the pizza accordingly and while she didn't seem impressed, there was a moment of relief when I had actual names of real people who were coming. I guess she wasn't as out of the loop as I had thought. My lack of talking about anyone or meeting up with anyone must have been a bit of a tip-off.

A quarter past seven I felt my heart beating and my face getting hot again. I hadn't thought to get their phone numbers or give them mine. They said they knew where my Aunt lived, and I just took their word on it.

Aunt June came and sat with me next to the fire I had lit, in hopes of creating some form of a beacon. With one hand rubbing my back, she gave me a sympathetic look. "They should be here any minute Honey. The roads leading out here can be a little tricky if you don't drive them often. I wouldn't be surprised if they took the wrong turn at the fork, they'll still loop back around, but it will take a little longer." I nodded in agreement knowing she was just trying to be supportive.

I was ready to be left alone and was grateful she needed to leave. "I know, they'll be here. And if they don't make it that's okay too. I really could use a break anyway. Do a little drawing and laundry." I tried to give her a reassuring smile, but I was growing increasingly upset. "I know you have your meeting tonight, and at this rate you're going to be late. I'll be here when you get back and you can tell me all about it over pizza."

She laughed that vibrant laugh, as her chandelier earrings flashed with the firelight. She was easy and had more love to give than I knew how to receive. "You're right. I should be heading out." She wrapped herself in her cloak, gave my hand a squeeze, and made her way to her car parked crooked in the gravel drive. As the engine turned over and the headlights came on, the second set of headlights came creeping through the driveway, all five dogs barking and dancing around this stranger's car as it parked beside the Nova.

Aunt June rolled her window down as she pulled out of her parking spot and waved to Samuel and Katie. Katie looked relieved as she got out of the driver's seat. I stood up and called for them feeling a rush of relief and gratitude.

Samuel had a cooler in his hand that he positioned in between him and Katie as they took their seats adjacent to me. One thing I could state with confidence about June's place was that her patio was magnificent. Partially covered to protect from the elements, but exposed enough to lay back and see the stars, there were string lights hung across the entire backyard, and the sound of the small waterfall was soothing. The furniture was in impeccable condition, especially considering the snow and animals.

"We're so sorry we're late, Samuel here was driving and insisted we take the left at the fork instead of the right, then we got completely turned around and I had to take over driving because he almost ran us into a ditch. Twice." Katie gave Samuel a dramatic look, and he handed her a beer from the cooler, making faces intended to mock her as he handed me one as well.

Aunt June was right, they took the wrong turn. I explained how tricky it was for me still and insisted no apology was necessary. As they looked around exchanging pleasantries about how nice the landscaping was, Samuel noticed the decorations and looked confused for a moment before he realized what they were for.

"Oh, man! Is it your birthday today?!" He stood up and gave me a stern pat on the back "Happy Birthday man I had no idea." Katie followed suit. "Why didn't you say anything, if we had known we would have gotten you a gift or something!" She stood up and gave me a hug as she wished me a happy birthday.

It was my first birthday without my parents, my mom would always try to throw me some elaborate surprise party but over the years it became more a social gathering for her and her friends than for me, so I quit showing and to little surprise, she didn't notice. Dad being out of town, he would always remember to call, but seldom made it home to celebrate. I would get a card and some money from the two of them to do with as I pleased. Every year they would ask me to bring Cameron over, but I never wanted to spend my birthdays with them, I always wanted to be out and about on my own. Now that they're gone, it didn't feel so different, but it didn't feel right.

Katie played music on her phone as we drank, ate pizza and talked for a few hours. It felt like we had been friends for years. They let me in on all the school-wide gossip and encouraged my distance from certain students as if it were my choice and not something inflicted on me.

By our last round of beers, Samuel had finally asked what I knew they were waiting all night to know.

"So, how did you wind up out here anyway?" Katie stepped on his foot as she stared at me in horror. Snatching his foot from the line of fire he redressed the question. "I just mean like, I've heard stories around campus but none of them are the same as the other, so I figured none of it would be real. I'm just curious how you got stuck out here in your junior year of high school."

It was very clear he didn't mean any ill will in his curiosity. My situation was a mystery to just about everyone. I took the moment as an opportunity to hopefully set the record straight.

After I told them what happened to my parents, and how I had to leave Detroit, I told them about my dad's line of work and how my parents met. Katie teared up while I spoke, Samuel kept himself together well but had a look in his eye that he understood.

I could feel my throat tightening as I spoke about it at certain points, but mostly I had gone over it enough times in my head I felt confident enough about it, thankfully my composure held.

As it turned out I wasn't alone. Samuel's parents left him with his grandparents for a weekend when he was eight and they never came back. He said they left to pursue a job opportunity and planned to be back for him once they got settled, then after about three years, the calls stopped coming. He heard from his Uncle in Florida that his parents moved to Connecticut and divorced around the time he quit getting calls. Neither of them ever came back and he never heard anything about them again.

His grandparents were his on his mother's side, and after the calls quit coming, they changed their number and moved as a form of exiling their daughter for what she did. Samuel said he was angry about them keeping her away from him, but as he got older, he realized what they did for him was more of a sacrifice for his goodwill than either of his parents would have made for him.

I know it's wrong to feel better about yourself knowing someone else is suffering too, but that was the first time I didn't feel entirely alone in months. Katie consoled him as he spoke, and I sat thinking about how great it must feel to have someone there for you the way they had each other. Cameron and I were always close, but even now it's only been a few months since I moved, and I haven't even received a birthday call from him. Which wasn't unlike him but stung none the less.

Aunt June pulled into the driveway as Samuel began to change the subject. We quickly put our empty beer cans back in his cooler. She waved as she walked inside, trying not to disturb what she assumed must be a successful gathering. Samuel and Katie stood up, ready to leave. I thanked them for coming and hanging out. We exchanged hugs which was a little strange for my taste, but the sentiment was nice. After swapping phone numbers, as I was readying myself to turn in for the night, Samuel asked if Katie and I were interested in crashing Taylors party.

"Come on guys, it's only ten o'clock. That party probably just got good, and I don't know about you Kenny, but I think getting out could be a fun way to end your birthday off right." Samuel was just short of putting me in the car on his own. And Katie encouraged it. She seemed to of caught a second wind at the idea of not letting her Friday night die out so early.

I was hesitant. Knowing how the kids at my school felt about me, especially Taylor. I hadn't shared that part of my experience with Samuel or Katie yet. "Let me go and make sure it's okay with my Aunt." They both hurried me along.

June may as well of been wearing binoculars. She was standing by the door staring at a tapestry she's had for decades pretending to be newly enticed by it as I walked in, I felt a chuckle deep down from the way she pretended she forgot I was even there and didn't hear me come in.

She was so encouraging of the invite you'd think she wanted to be rid of me. I grabbed my coat and headed out to Samuels car, Katie insisted on driving again, which I didn't mind considering Samuel never denied the 'almost ran into a ditch twice' accusation.

Chapter Eleven

Taylors home looked like something out of a magazine. The driveway was a mile long and had a gate propped open at the entrance, leading to a house three stories high with a two-story wrap around porch. The shutters were navy blue, to match the door, everything else was stark white. Katie pulled in and parked under an oak tree between a dozen other cars and we made our way inside. Samuel and Katie were both greeted generously as we walked through the front door, considering the sideways glances my accompanying them generated. I felt a spotlight on myself. They were well-liked by most of the school and my showing to Taylor's party with them must have been a form of social defiance.

The kitchen centralized the gathering, Katie passed drinks around between the three of us as her friend Sierra approached us with a look of confusion.

"Katie!" Sierra hugged her friend, never taking her eyes off me. "How's it going? I didn't think you two would show. Samuel, good to see you here too." Her glare broke as Samuel picked her up in a grand hug.

"Sierra meet our friend Kenny. He moved

here recently from Detroit and it's his birthday today. Sam and I thought he could use a little outing." Katie gave her friend a look daring her to question a motive.

"Hi, Kenny. I'm Sierra. I didn't know you all were friends?" Sierra said with a curious tone smiling at Katie. "Well, it's nice to meet you. Katie – would you come with me? Fred is here and he brought that girl. I think I need some assistance running interference."

Katie agreed and gave Samuel a look that screamed 'Save Me' as Sierra pulled her through the crowd by her hand.

Samuel laughed, seemingly enjoying the torment his friend was enduring. He and I went on for a while discussing trivial things when Taylor made her way into the kitchen. Word seemed to spread of my presence the way she and her entourage cleared the room.

"Oh Samuel, again with the strays." Taylor was leaning into Samuel's chest as she glared at me, claiming her territory.

Samuel pushed her back gently enough to not cause trouble but stern enough to make his point just as Katie rejoined our ranks. Almost as if she could sense the tension from wherever she was before, she didn't miss a beat. Barely looking in Taylor's direction Katie took the first shot.

"Taylor. It's almost midnight and you're still up? Did you finally kick the Xanax habit, or have you just built a better tolerance since Prom?" She positioned herself on the kitchen counter between Samuel and I, grabbed a beer I wasn't sure was even hers off the counter, and took a swig.

I could feel my throat get tight again, the feeling of being somewhere I wasn't welcome, in a home I didn't recognize and in a town I knew little of. Taylor stammered, but only for a moment. With a smug look on her face and her arms crossed she took a step towards Katie.

"Little Katie brought her claws. Been a while since we've seen those. Careful, or your mom might send you away again. Would be a crying shame if she caught word you were out drinking and picking fights."

Katie's poker face faltered to a split second of sheer hatred and anger. Samuel stepped between the two of them "Thanks for the drinks and warm wishes Taylor, but we were actually just leaving." While polite enough, Samuel had a tone of agitation. Taylor smiled and looked to her crew behind her who had been standing there silently watching the whole debacle through.

"Now, you don't need to leave, I'll be nice. I promise." Taylor unfolded her arms and put a hand lovingly on Samuel's arm. "But this party is a plus 1, and if you're bringing Ms. Priss along – I'm afraid," She trailed off as her hand dropped from Samuel's arm, and her eyebrows raised in my direction. "I'm sorry. Who are you again?"

I felt my face flush with heat and my eyes

get watery. I was never good at confrontation, or as the center of attention. And right now, I was in the hot seat and all eyes were on me.

"This is Kenny, Taylor." Samuel rolled his eyes. "He's with me. Do we have a problem with that?"

Taylor accepted his challenge. "As a matter of fact, we do."

Katie popped down from the counter and locked arms with me. "Let's go gentlemen. Seems the party's gotten a little stale."

Taylor waved us off with a smile on her face and the party seemed to resume as it was before we even made it out of the front door.

"I'm sorry you guys. I should have told you before, Taylor and I aren't exactly on good terms." I felt choked up, embarrassed by the scene that just unfolded and the awkward situation I put Katie and Samuel in. The only two people I had connected with since moving here and I blew it the first night.

Katie looked at me through the rearview mirror as we pulled down the mile-long driveway and refused to accept my apology. "Taylor is the literal worst. No one likes Taylor and she doesn't like anyone either. Her parents are loaded, that's the only reason people even associate with her. What happened between the two of you anyway?"

I explained how June tried to set us up over the first week I was here and how it went up in smoke in the worst way. Katie and Samuel both ganged up on me with words of encouragement and support, clearly taking my side in the matter.

"You think that's bad?" Samuel laughed at himself "You should hear what went down with her and Katie."

Katie gave him a look from the driver's side that implied she didn't want to share but did so anyway as we pulled onto my street. "Taylor and I were really close through middle school. Until freshman year she started dating a sophomore, and all of a sudden, she just started being really rude and nasty. So, I quit hanging out with her."

Katie's voice trailed off for a moment and her head cocked to the side. Like she was struggling with whether she should continue her story. "Then when they broke up a couple of months later, he started hitting on me between classes. I wasn't interested and made that perfectly clear to him, but that wasn't good enough for her. Taylor started this awful rumor that I had an STD, and when I confronted her about it, things got a little out of hand."

The tone in her voice lifted toward the end, implying there was more to the story that she wasn't as embarrassed about as she initially let on. A smile crept along her face and a slight chuckle came to. "Basically, I beat the shit out of her with an umbrella. The police were called, parents got involved. Her parents agreed not to press charges if my parents enrolled me at a different school. So, my parents sent me to a boarding school to finish my freshman year. By the end of summer leading to sophomore year things had calmed down and our parents came to an understanding and I got to come back to our lovely Carbondale High."

Samuel cheered Katie on and bowed to her playfully from the passenger seat. I was curious why Samuel would be so encouraging of his best friend's distaste for a girl he supposedly had a crush on. As I got out of the car and thanked them for the evening, I mustered up the ability to ask.

Samuel shrugged and laughed "Hey man, Taylors a grade 'A' Bitch. But she's hot." He extended his fist out to me in some form of an attempt to bond. I smiled and declined the gesture; on the basis I couldn't understand the junction. He didn't take offense.

I went back inside and made my way upstairs to my room. The whole week leading to that night was stressful, I was beyond ready for bed.

Chapter Twelve

Over the following months, Aunt June and I spent almost every evening I wasn't with my new friends, working in her studio. She started a new charity event project for the American Cancer Society set for Spring at The House in town. It was incredible watching her work, she was so patient when things didn't go according to plan with her sculptures and her painting was intensively thoughtful. Every brush stroke seemed to serve a purpose.

I worked alongside her on my mixed media canvas pieces and she was supportive where I lacked the support myself. There were several times I would throw my brushes across the room in frustration and each time she would look at me and suggest I throw them at my work as opposed to her studio. At first, it seemed critical and angry, I would storm out of the studio and protest my work for the evening. Over time I came to understand, she was never talking about my brushes, she was talking about throwing my frustrations at my work quite literally.

She was already in the studio one night as I made my way in after an evening with Samuel at the pizzeria. I was in an exceptionally good mood and wanted to try and get my most recent piece done, even if it took all night. June's gallery opening was in a week so I knew she would be pulling long hours too and I was looking forward to telling her about my night. The studio was poorly lit and smelled of weed and whiskey. The combination wasn't uncommon when she dove so deep into her work, but it just seemed different that night.

Aunt June was slumped back in her seat, staring at her completed piece. She had constructed a life-size sculpture of a naked weeping woman on her knees, one hand on the ground and the other reaching out above her as if she were grasping for a hand to help her to her feet. I watched that project come to life over the prior months, but something about seeing it at that moment was like I was seeing it for the first time. It was finished. Whatever final touches June had done worked miracles on the figure. The woman appeared broken down, weak, lost, and desperate. It was breath-taking.

I let out a quiet gasp and she jumped to her feet; aware she was no longer alone. It looked like she'd been crying. "I'm sorry, Aunt June I didn't mean to intrude. I can come back later." I started walking backward, feeling dreadful as if I overstepped my boundaries. My Aunt and I have never had a conventional relationship, she was always open and more of a friend than a parental figure. It was easy to sometimes forget I was her ward.

Aunt June straightened herself out, with dry red and puffy eyes she walked to me with a smile on her face and arms outward for a hug. "No no no, don't be silly. You have perfect timing. I have finally finished her." She put her arm around my shoulders and stared at her work admiringly in the way I wanted to. But I was more worried about her than anything else. She was all I had left. My grandparents had been long gone; my parents were gone. My dad had no siblings and June was it from my mother's side. I knew it wasn't my business, but I needed to make sure she was okay. To make sure we were okay. "What's going on Aunt June? You look like you've been crying." I felt weak getting the words out. Even if something was wrong, I wasn't sure I would be of any use. I hardly knew how to handle my own problems, much less anyone else's.

"Oh, my sweet Kenny. Everything is fine. I don't mean to worry you. This sculpture means a lot to me, I must have gotten carried away." She gave me a reassuring smile and walked me to my canvas, sat me down, and began setting up my station before continuing to speak or allowing me to say anything.

"My art expresses my triumphs and submissions equally. In art, much like in life, the most beautiful things come from a balance of light and dark. One without the other means nothing. How can you ever know happiness if you have never felt sadness? How can you know hatred if you've never known love?" She took a step back as I looked cautiously at my canvas, unsure of what she was trying to say.

"People appreciate the art they connect to. The art they can feel move something inside of them. Deep-rooted thoughts and desires. Art is a reflection of the artist, and the artist is a reflection of the world they know. I've kept quiet long enough and allowed you the opportunity to heal in whichever way you felt best. But you haven't spoken about your parents since you arrived months ago. I support what you need to do, but I can't sit by and continue watching you pretend everything is okay. Because it's not and hasn't been for some time."

She removed my half-completed canvas from the tabletop easel and replaced it with a clean one twice its size. I was frozen, sinking like quicksand through the floorboards beneath me. My throat dry, its walls closing in on themselves as my eyes stuck open in horror, filled with tears. Aunt June laid a careful hand on my shoulder from behind me, my body shattering into a million pieces at the thought of my parents. If she noticed, she wouldn't let it be known.

"You don't have to talk about it if you don't want to, but you need to do something. Or the pain will fester itself so deep inside of you, you will never learn to move on." Her hand slipped off my shoulder and she stood still for a moment, I couldn't bring myself to turn around to face her. "I miss Olivia Kenny. Your mom. She was my best friend. She was wild, free and strong, and had this kindness in her that could bring even the cruelest of men to their knees. I envied her for it in our earlier days." Her voice cracked. Causing her to pause.

I had been doing well, I was happy for the first time since my parents could last stand to be in the same room together. I had friends and hobbies, she didn't know what she was talking about, I wasn't bottling anything. There was a sense of her patronizing me, trying to console me on something I didn't ask to be consoled about. I was in a great mood, I wanted to talk to her, about everything that was going right in my life, and she spoiled it. Now I was angry.

That anger took hold of me and I turned to look at June as my voice carried words that didn't feel like my own.

"My mom was not a kind woman. She hardly spoke to me for years leading to last summer. My dad never came home because she was such a miserable person. She was mad about everything. Nothing he ever did made her happy. So, whatever 'Olivia' you think you know, you don't." Hatred pulsed through my veins, the feeling familiar and unsettling.

I wanted desperately to storm out of the studio, stuck with my limbs temporarily paralyzed, and ridged I was forced to sit and wait the episode out. June closed her eyes as a single tear fell from her eye. Just as quickly as my temper had risen, it dissipated. Instantly filled with regret, I wanted to apologize. My anger was misplaced. June had done nothing wrong, she wanted to help. Or maybe she wasn't thinking of me at all, maybe she was the one who needed to talk. Maybe this whole time she had been bottling it up herself, and she just needed someone to talk to who would understand.

"Aunt June, I'm so sorry, that wasn't fair." I turned back around in my chair, holding my head in my hands in front of the canvas. Tears streaming down my arms. She took a seat next to me at the table, and gently pulled my hands from my face, cradling them in her own.

"Don't apologize Kenny. You're right." Her voice was calm and stable. "I don't know the Olivia you do. Because I never gave her a chance. She reached out to me a few times over the years I was gone, but I was too caught up in myself to appreciate that for what it was. I should have tried to be there. And I wasn't. I am the one who should be sorry. Should the time come, and you would like to talk about it, I would love to hear about the woman you know and share with you the woman I knew long ago. I think we both would enjoy that." She released her hold allowing my hands to ground themselves complacently on the desk, I was exhausted from the conversation and wanted it to be over. "Whenever you're ready."

She walked woefully out of the studio. I sat mesmerized at the clean canvas before me, my mind spinning, a pang of confusion and frustration shot through my body. I threw the canvas across the studio as a scream came from deep inside of me. I stood in place, fighting back tears and lumbering through my resentment and loneliness. I was tired of fighting. My knees gave out from under me as I came crashing to the ground, I gasped for air as sawdust from the floor stirred and cut my throat. My parents were gone, and they weren't coming back.

After some time, as I laid on the studio floor, flat on my back staring blankly at the ceiling, I dried the tears from my eyes and retrieved the discarded canvas. The feeling of a two-ton weight lifted off my chest gave me a second wind. There was a hole ripped through the center of the canvas where it struck the stretcher on the other end of the room. I felt hollow with guilt. Ruining something that, before my frustration took the best of it, was in perfectly good condition. Then the irony struck, the canvas and I had something in common. For the first time in my life, I had felt purpose in my art.

I placed the canvas against the wall and sat on the ground. Level with the dirt of the world, right where I deserved to be for feeling such resentment toward my parents. They were dead and I hated them for it. My work started in dark watercolors to interpret the death I couldn't escape, imprinting the auras of my parents on either side of the gaping gash in the canvas. Empty and hollow. Using an unwashed muslin cloth, I created borders surrounding the laceration, as a representation of my isolation and wilted green wax paper butterflies on the inside of those constructed borders. One for Aunt June, the second for Samuel, and the third for Katie.

I spent almost six hours that night working on it and felt compelled to complete it. With every splash of red, onyx and plum I could feel myself grow lighter and weaker all at once. Just after midnight I went into the house and headed straight for bed. I could hear the singing bowl coming from June's room, which meant she was still awake and meditating.

As I laid on top of my comforter, too tired to pull the sheets back, I thought self-consciously about my time in the studio.

Chapter Thirteen

Aunt June saw my finished canvas the next day and encouraged me to donate it to the gallery for the Lymphoma Charity event. I was skeptical at first, it felt wrong to put something out there that took so much out of me. I had reassurance of my work before when my piece sold in Detroit to an anonymous buyer, but when I discovered the anonymous buyer was June, it depleted my confidence a little. She may not have been around and by no means did she need to buy it, but it still felt a little humiliating that my one highest achievement was a farse. No exceedingly talented artists became famous because their families bought their work, unfortunately.

I gave in, deciding it was for a good cause, and if it didn't sell, I could retrieve it from the gallery wall and lock it away forever.

The morning of the event, Aunt June and I went to The House early to get an unfiltered look at the work donated. There were dozens of artists from across the West Coast who participated, and the walls were already littered with artists' displays by the time I arrived. I found my wall space, stark white and protected only by a single stanchion. After hanging my canvas on its hook, I took a step back and got a picture of it in its place. It was my second gallery piece and by far a much more professional show than the one in Detroit a few years before. The caterer wasn't due to be there for a few more hours, then the guests an hour after that, which left us with more time than I was sure to do with.

Aunt June encouraged everyone to head to the café across the street for coffee, though only a few agreed to join us. We went across the street, ordered lattes and scones, and sat around getting to know one another. Samantha was a photographer from Denver and was the most talkative of any of us, but I liked her the best. She was only several years older than I was and had traveled the world for her work. It was incredible hearing her stories.

One of the gentlemen who joined us, Bennett, was a local of Carbondale that June knew well. He was roughly Aunt June's age and dabbled in Mixed Media Art as I did. We chatted for a while on and off about it, but it seemed he wasn't any more vested in it than I was. He worked at the library in town and his art was more of a hobby than anything else.

Then there was Curtis, a little younger than my Aunt and much older than me, he had flown in from Seattle. Curtis was friendly enough, when I asked why he would come all the way to Carbondale, Colorado for a charity event he explained his wife had been diagnosed with Lymphoma and she passed a few years before. They lived in a town not too far from Carbondale at the time so he was well acquainted with the area, but after her passing, he couldn't stand to be there anymore and left. She apparently had always wanted to move to Seattle, so he went for her.

I had that same feeling again that I felt when Samuel told me about his parents leaving him with his grandparents and never coming back for him. Sympathetic, but grateful. To not be so alone in having your loved ones leave you behind.

That evening at the gala, Samuel and Katie came dressed to the nines, as did everyone else. They came to support me and Aunt June, who they had grown wildly close to over the winter. Katie and June had a lot in common, apparently Katie's interest in psychology complimented Aunt June's knack for human persuasion. Katie found it fascinating watching Aunt June function through life and hearing her stories. Samuel felt a motherly tenderness from June he seemed to lack at home with his grandparents, and June had a soft spot for him and his excitability.

Curtis came to see me by the drink station about my display and showed a great deal of interest in it. There were a few people who asked about the inspiration behind it and I couldn't bring myself to share that yet, so I thought best to step away and tried to avoid too deep of a conversation about it. Forgetting that my name was on the plaque beside it and that I made the fortune of meeting Curtis earlier, he had no trouble placing me with the piece.

We talked about it, against my better judgment, but there was something almost parental about Curtis. He was the strong silent type; my dad was like that. Perfectly friendly but never offered up more information about himself than directly necessary. I shared my story with him, about my parents' accident and how I had felt particularly alone the night I made that canvas. He had a glimmer in his eye that would suggest he understood the feeling, but he didn't offer any condolences, only praise for my ability to translate my emotion to canvas. It was incredibly kind and a relief that he didn't try and console me for my loss, but kept the conversations focus on his appreciation for the art I created.

My painting sold that night for several hundred dollars to Bennet, the man who lived on the outskirts of town. He requested I sign my work before he left and shook my hand.

I did it. I finally completed a piece of work for the first time since I moved here. And it felt so relieving to know it was sold for a good cause, we raised nearly five thousand dollars that night for the American Cancer Society.

The gallery received a plaque in the mail a few weeks later thanking them for hosting the event. And Aunt June made me a plaque of my own in her workshop.

"This is for you Sweet Kenny," She handed me the plaque with a look of complete pleasure with herself and a hint of pride. "To commemorate your very first legitimate gallery sale and charitable donation."

I laughed at the brilliance of it and thanked her as she helped me hang it in my room by the doorway.

Chapter Fourteen

As summer approached, I took to more outdoor activities. We were surrounded by forests and hiking trails I hadn't explored, and it was time for me to experience it. Growing up in the city I didn't have many opportunities to find out if I was the outdoorsy type, being in Carbondale the options were endless. A trailhead down the road from June's house lead to a creek and small waterfall, I would bring the dogs with me on the weekends and walk the stream about a mile down and head back. On particularly hot days, I would swim in the creek. The trees standing higher than any skyscraper shielded me from the sun.

Samuel took Katie and I kayaking at Avalanche Creek later in the summer when the intensity of the Forks River Tourism died down. Having never been before, they guided me through the how-to and I hit the water. They chose the easiest and safest river nearby knowing I was new to the sport, and it was the most exhilarating experience of my life.

Samuel spent a lot of time at football training camp and Katie was volunteering at the psychiatrist's office in town a few hours a week to beef up her resume.

Which left me home to work in the studio. The sale I made at the charity gala gave me a fresh sense of confidence and control over myself and my life. I took Aunt June's advice and started directing my anger and frustrations, as well as my celebrations, toward the canvas and I was finishing projects left and right.

The library downtown agreed to let me display and sell my art, after signing a contract agreeing to pay them a five percent fee, I started filling my allotted areas almost immediately. I wasn't in it for the money so much as I was because I loved the work, and the validation when someone bought a piece. So, paying a fee, especially such a small one was a fair deal in my eyes. My work didn't sell often, so I created a schedule for display. Any piece that was left hanging for longer a month would be removed, and I would instead post them online and try that market for them. They were in reasonable demand online, mostly in California and Maine. A few here and there, nothing to get a big head about but enough to feel accomplished.

With Summer at an end and my Eighteenth birthday only several weeks away, my sense of mortality crept to the front of my mind. Senior year brings the end of my time in Carbondale, and I was expected to move back to Detroit, my parent's condo was paid off and sitting there, waiting for me to come back. As was my dad's company. Despite my parents leaving me an inheritance that would set me up for several years without working', it didn't seem right to ignore the responsibilities I had laid out in front of me.

I received a letter through my parent's trust over the summer from Dad's board of directors, expressing their sympathies and anticipation for my joining them that next year. I never felt drawn to his line of work, but I always wanted to travel as he would and the money was hard to turn down. Not to mention, I inherited the company. Walking away from such a generous hand would be cruel. But now, in Carbondale with my Aunt and my friends and my art, I can't tell if that's still something I want to do. I do miss Cameron, we keep in touch though not as often. He has been planning on going to Michigan State, so he would still be close by when I returned home.

Samuel and Katie were both leaving the state after graduation which was hard to accept. We had grown close and despite that most of my classmates had come around to me at school, I didn't have many other friends. So it would be me, Aunt June and the dogs. In a small town with one movie theater and no mall for miles. My employment opportunities were bleak as well, I had no interest in working at a local shop for the rest of my life and college was never an interest either. Aunt June made a living on her art because she established herself and her clientele over the decades. My pieces have sold just enough so that I didn't need a summer job or to ask June for money until my trust is released, not a dollar more. Which meant I needed something feasible.

Chapter Fifteen

Summer came and went, and my senior year of high school started, It was unfair how quickly the time had gone, I spent weeks mulling over my options for post-graduation and decided I would move back to Detroit after all. I was happy in Carbondale, but everyone else had plans to get on with their lives soon, I needed to do the same.

Aunt June decorated the house again in celebration of my birthday and invited Samuel and Katie over herself. They were all ready to the house by the time I got there. I stopped to replace a canvas that was sold earlier that day at the library which caused me to run behind.

Katie brought a friend of hers I met a couple of times in passing, but I was surprised to see her there. Luckily, she didn't notice my reserves about her attendance.

"Happy birthday Kenny! I'm not positive you remember me, but we met a while back at the café, I was there with Katie when you came in?" Her voice trailed off quizzically before I gave her a nod of remembrance. Of course I remembered her, how could

I forget? "I'm Alana. Thanks so much for letting me come along." She gave me a gentle hug that smelled of linen and rain. She had long dark curly hair and amber eyes, I stumbled for the words for a moment before catching myself.

"No, absolutely. Thank you for coming. It's so great to see you." I felt heat rise to my face in embarrassment and busied myself looking for a glass in the cupboard before anyone could notice.

Almost anyone, Katie must have caught a glimpse as I turned away and took over without missing a beat. "Well, Alana! Let June and I show you the rest of the house, I'm sure Samuel and Kenny have a few things to catch up on before we can get this party started." Katie gave me a look to get myself together as she guided Alana and a confused Aunt June out of the kitchen.

I stood there and shot a glare at Samuel with a smirk on his face leaning against the counter eating chips. "Dude, why didn't you guys tell me she was coming?" They'd known for months I had a crush on her ever since we first met at the café and I hadn't stopped thinking about her since.

Samuel caught up to the conversation and almost choked. "Oh, yea. I told Katie we should tell you, but she said she wasn't sure Alana would make it and knew you'd panic. Which turns out she was right." He let out a chuckle. "I'll let you in on a little secret though, turns out she's pretty into you too."

My heart skipped a beat and I tried to collect myself to play it cool.

Later that evening after the pizza was demolished and the fire died out Alana said her goodbyes for the evening and as she was walking toward her car in the drive Samuel gave me a nudge to ask her out, so I excused myself and tried to catch her before she got into her car.

"Alana!" I waved at her and slowed my pace as she turned around, acknowledging my calling for her. She was in a t-shirt and jeans, her curly hair pulled back into a low ponytail and I was nearly left breathless by the sight of her in the moonlight.

She laughed when I took a moment too long to gather my thoughts and picked up the conversation we weren't yet having.

"Thank you again for inviting me over, this was fun. And your Aunts house is amazing." Her smile made my stomach twist inside itself.

If I went back to Samuel without good news, I would never hear the end of it. I was sure of that.

"I'm happy you could make it." I grinned nervously, unsure how far I could push my luck. "Listen, I was curious if you might be interested in going out with me sometime. Maybe. If you're not busy. If you are busy it's no big deal or anything, I just figured I would ask." I began to ramble, which made her laugh.

"Kenny, I would love that." She put her hand out requesting my phone so she could leave me her number. "Text me tomorrow if you'd like and we can make plans." She handed my phone back and waved goodbye still smiling as she opened her car door.

By the time I realized what had just happened, Samuel came up behind me and put his hand on my shoulder.

"You okay Bro?" There was laughter in his tone. "You look like you just saw a ghost."

I mustered out the only words I could find.

"She said yes."

Chapter Sixteen

The morning after my birthday I got a call from my parents' lawyer to discuss the inheritance, including the condo in Detroit. I knew the call was coming and I had been preparing myself for weeks. I didn't want their money and I certainly didn't want our old home. There were too many memories there. I hadn't been home since I packed my bags for Colorado and thinking about going back made sick with anxiety.

A meeting was set to meet the lawyer a week from that day in Detroit to finalize the paperwork and sign the documents. I needed to pack and let the school know of my upcoming absence.

That afternoon during lunch I told Katie and Samuel about my coming trip. They were supportive, though Samuel had quite a string of suggestions for what I could do with the money I was left. It was clear he still harbored resentment towards his parents for leaving him behind all those years ago, but he never allowed it to interfere with his life. He made choices every day to still be kind to everyone around him, to still smile and laugh.

Of all the times we had spoken, when I would go

off the rails in anger and regret, he would sit there and allow that for me. He would never fuel my fire, he would never compare our situations, he would never hold it against me. He showed the strength and compassion I aspired to. I worked hard every day to be half the man I recognized Samuel to be, while he had his faults, he showed grace in a disgraceful situation and I respected that beyond measure.

Katie habitually side-eyed Samuel when he would commentate inappropriately, but it was clear she felt the same way about him as I did. She would never hold his mannerisms against him because she knew even better than I did that he was doing his best in an unfair situation.

They offered to come with me, as did Aunt June the night before when I shared my fear of walking through the door of the place that was once my home. I felt relief at the thought of all three of them being with me, but the trip would be painstakingly boring and depressing. I couldn't in good conscience submit them to something like that. Despite my reservations, Katie and Samuel insisted they should go, and after mild hesitation, I agreed to let them help me through it. Aunt June was happy to hear I wouldn't be going alone and asked if I would mind her staying behind. The thought of leaving the dogs unattended or boarded during our absence was stressful for her and knowing I would have my friends with me gave me the confidence to let her sit it out.

Over the last year and a half Aunt June took time

away from the studio to teach me to drive, then just a matter of weeks before my birthday she took me to get my license. Being raised in the city it wasn't much of a necessity but living in Carbondale you couldn't very well survive without it. Having my license served me especially well the Friday before my trip, I took Aunt June's car and picked Alana up for our first date.

Alana lived down the street from the library in a house about the size of Aunt Junes. It was yellow with white shutters and trim, and an exceptionally busy garden tracing the length of the stairs to the porch. I could smell the lavender still despite the fall weather breaking to winter as I stood by the front door waiting for her to answer.

She was wearing a dark green sweater dress and nude flats, her curly hair falling delicately over her shoulder. I knew I would never forget the feeling of awe that overtook me. She was hard not to notice, even in her jeans and t-shirts, but that dress I knew would haunt me forever.

I suggested dinner and a movie for the evening and insisted she pick the restaurant. She acted coy when suggesting pizza only to burst with enthusiasm as I agreed and pulled onto the street. We were over-dressed for the pizzeria, I felt wildly uncomfortable in my button-down shirt tucked into my khakis, but she wore the attention well. If she sensed the people staring, you would never know. She was quiet and polite. Her smile lit up the room and I knew I would do anything to hear her laugh again and again.

She told me about her dreams to be a fashion designer and wanting to create her own clothing line. She had already been accepted to the Fashion Institute of Technology in New York. Watching Alana talk about her dream career was what being high must have felt like. She radiated warmth and the look in her eye told me she would have it all one day.

At the end of the evening, I drove her back to her home and walked her to the door. My skin felt hot again, my palms wet, clutching the keys between my fingers. As I tried to stumble through my pleasantries about the evening Alana leaned in and kissed me gently. My toes went numb and she took the breath from me as she pulled back.

On the drive home I kept replaying our night in my head, and that kiss. I knew she was leaving after graduation, as were my only friends, as was I. It was crazy to want to see her again, but crazier not to. She was perfect.

Aunt June was awake when I walked in, her singing bowl humming from her room had come to a stop as I shut the door. She came bursting through her curtains with a look of yearning. "*So*?!" Her hands waving in an attempt to produce information from thin air. "How did it go?" She pulled up a chair in the dining room never looking away from me.

I couldn't help but smile. I don't think I had stopped since I picked Alana up hours ago. "It went just fine Aunt June." I turned around to head to my room laughing, knowing I had all the power over her at that moment. She wanted details but I wasn't going to cave and give them up so easily. It was almost embarrassing how much I adored Alana, talking about it was well out of my comfort. "I'm going to bed now, I'll see you in the morning!"

"Oh! Kenny!" Aunt June was snickering. I know she worried about me often, and for me to do something so normal as going on a date must have brought her relief.

The next morning by the time I finished my breakfast, she squeezed out every detail about the night before. Some of which I didn't intend on sharing at all. It was strange feeling so comfortable talking to her, I knew I could be candid with my friends, but I hadn't been that way with June before. She reminded me of my mom from when I was young. Before things changed.

Aunt June was supportive of my relationship with Alana but was quick to remind me that at the end of the school year everything would change, and suggested I sit with Alana to discuss that sooner rather than later.

I knew she was right, but I also knew that Alana was aware I was going back to Detroit already, and I clearly knew she was going to New York. What was the purpose of having a conversation about something that was still several months away?

I chose to play it out day by day and if the need arose to have that talk, then we would. But for now, I just wanted to enjoy our time together.

The next day I boarded the plane with Katie and Samuel, they were bickering their usual amount between questions about my date. I knew Katie had to of already gotten word considering she was close friends with Alana, but Samuel came across as clueless as he surely was and teased me the whole flight about being so taken with her.

Chapter Seventeen

Neither Samuel nor Katie been outside of Colorado before, so visiting Detroit was a big deal to them. I planned on taking them to all the best tourist stops while we were there, including the Institute of Art. I was ecstatic to see what new exhibits they had. The local gallery in Carbondale was great but it wasn't the same. I was limited to local work in Carbondale, and I missed the abundance of different works from around the world.

As we got off the elevator to the condo, I saw a woman I didn't recognize unlocking Camille's door.

"Hi, I'm Kenny, I used to live next door." I felt inclined to see who this woman was. Camille and I weren't friends by any stretch, but if someone was taking advantage of her home I wanted to know. "Are you Camille's daughter?"

She turned to look at me, reasonably confused. "Oh, hi Kenny, nice to meet you, I'm Shannon." She extended her hand as Camille's front door crept open behind her. The lace curtains and decorative art were no longer there. They had all been replaced with chrome figures and black furniture, a very drastic change since I had seen it last. "I'm sorry to say I don't actually know who Camille is. I just moved in a couple of months back, so I assume she must have been the one who lived here before." Her face softened and she looked down at her feet.

I felt my throat get tight but managed to ask if she knew where Camille had moved to, knowing deep down she hadn't moved at all. Shannon was kind enough in explaining what little she knew about the woman I grew up across the hall from. Camille passed in her sleep in the spring and her family put her condo for sale at a low price in hopes of softening the blow of someone having died in it.

Everyone was dying. I couldn't seem to escape it.

I thanked Shannon for her time and wished her well, guiding my friends across the hall to what I used to call home. My hands were shaking trying to unlock the door. Katie placed her hand on my shoulder and took the key to unlock it for me. It had been almost two years since I was there last. Not much had changed, my parents' attorney allotted a housekeeper to stop by once a month to check on the place and keep it tidy to not let it rot. They weren't sure how long I would be gone and needed to protect the integrity of anything valuable listed in the will.

I gave Katie and Samuel the tour, each of them claimed a bedroom for their stay. Though ultimately, we all slept in the living room when the time came. I couldn't bring myself to sleep there, too many memories and not enough answered questions. My friends had both put in their best efforts over the few days we were there to keep my mind off everything but surrounded by my family pictures on the walls made it hard to escape.

The lawyer came by that following morning, papers sprawled across the dining room table. Each needing a signature for their own purposes. I was left enough money to live for years with no other income. Add that to what I was entitled in back pay and future payments from Dad's company, I may never need to work again.

Once all of the papers were signed and stamped, I insisted on keeping good on my promise to take Samuel and Katie to see the city. We didn't make it back until nearly three in the morning, which I was grateful for. The exhaustion had allowed me to finally sleep.

When we woke that next day, we packed our bags and headed for the airport to go back home. Being there was hard but having Katie and Samuel there made everything all the better. I wouldn't have been able to do it without them and I had no idea how I would repay them.

Aunt June met us at the airport and drove Katie and Samuel to their homes, pulling into our driveway around ten that evening. After getting settled back in the house, I sat in the dining room next to June.

We sat in silence for a moment, waiting for the other to speak when she took the lead.

"How was the trip?" The tone in her voice delicate and reassuring.

I sat on my hands, unsure what else to do with them as I stared at the salt and pepper shakers in front of me. Maintaining my line of vision and focusing on my breathing I spoke.

"I think I'm ready." The certainty in my voice presenting faulty confidence. "To talk. About Mom." I looked up at June from the corner of my eye, her face pressed with concern, quickly softened to gratitude.

"I would really like that." She placed her hand on the table, prompting me to slide her mine. "Tell me about her."

We spoke for hours about my childhood and how close Mom and I were, the inside jokes and fights. The stories Mom told me about her childhood and how she seldom mentioned her sister. I told her about the day I came home from school and she was gone, the day everything changed.

Aunt June shared the same stories my mom told me, but from her perspective.

"You would never guess it, but your mom used to be the most loud, passionate and asinine person I ever knew." Aunt June's tearfulness from moments before dissipated as she erupted in laughter. The thought of my mom being anything other than obsessively punctual and proper was bizarre. She continued to tell me about the numerous times in their earlier years Mom would get them both into trouble at home by keeping June out past curfew, and about the time Mom packed a bag her senior year of high school and hitchhiked across the country.

Mom was the older sister, so their parents drilled down twice as hard on June when she would act out. June swears my Mom's final adolescent stunt of cross-country hitchhiking is what made her want to travel the world. She wanted to be like her sister.

When the stories began to fade out, and emotional exhaustion got the best of us we decided to call it a night. As I excused myself from the table, Aunt June took my hand again. Urging me to sit for a moment longer.

"Kenny, I need you to know, your parents loved you more than anything in the world. I think your mom lost herself somewhere over the years and your dad wasn't equipped to handle that, so he hid from it. It doesn't mean they weren't good people, or that they didn't love you. You have been given a horribly unfair hand in your life, and I am so sorry for that. You deserve so much more in life. And I know, one day, you will have it." She squeezed my hand gently before letting go. "I love you Kenny. And I am so happy to have you here with me."

A sense of pious peace washed over me. "I love you too." I gave Aunt June a grateful smile and made my way up the stairs to bed. I was' expected back at school the next day.

Chapter Eighteen

By winter break Katie and Samuel had gotten acceptance letters to the schools of their choice. Alana and I had gotten serious by Spring, she was talking about me moving to New York with her. She knew I was planning on going back to Detroit to work at my Dad's firm, but she also knew deep down I had no interest in accounting. The sentiment was sweet, but realistically if I were leaving Carbondale it would be for Detroit, not New York. We played with the idea of her going to school in Detroit, but that plan died out before it even began. She was New York-bound, I was headed for Detroit and we knew what that meant for the two of us.

Senior year came and went. Graduation was upon us, and the air was different. Our graduating class consisted of almost one hundred students yet even being so few, it was as if the whole town was shifted into a new light. A handful of my classmates had positions lined up for them in Carbondale with no reason or desire to move away or go to a university. Most everyone else was University bound, scattering across the country pursuing their own dreams.

Alana and I agreed to do our best after graduation to try and keep the relationship going, even knowing it was a pipe dream we had every intention of giving it our best try. It broke Aunt June's heart accepting that Alana and I may not be running off into the sunset as she had hoped.

We met the day before graduation and spoke amicably about going our separate ways. She was feeling a lot of pressure about the program she was enrolled in. Which I understood fully, I was feeling a lot of pressure with going to work in Detroit, to sit in the same chair my dad once sat in. Trying to fill those shoes. It had to end between us, it was disappointing and relieving all at once to do it then, rather than in several months after living in denial about the hardships of long-distance relationships. We agreed to keep in touch and made haphazard agreements to visit one another.

There was a graduation party at Taylor's house the day after the ceremony, and in the emotional mix of everyone saying goodbye, I seemed to of made the guest list. Samuel, Katie and I met at my place before and reminisced on the first time we all got together. Sitting around that same fireplace, prepping to head to that same large white house with navy shutters for the last time.

It was nice to know that not everything had changed, not yet.

Chapter Nineteen

Three Years Later

My friends and I all moved away over the few weeks following graduation. Samuel Katie and I kept in close touch and my friendship with Cameron picked up almost right where it was left years before. I took the position that was left for me at my dad's accounting firm, learning the tricks of the trade over the last few years, and preparing to take my seat as CEO.

I sold my parents' condo and bought a small house on a quaint piece of land just outside of Detroit. The commute wasn't ideal, but the space was worth it. I converted the garage into a full-time studio where my projects had completely taken over and I continued selling my work online.

Overall, I was doing well, but I missed Carbondale. I missed the air and the town. I missed the hiking trails and most of all Aunt June. We kept in contact, though the calls got fewer over that last year. I kept making promises to visit, but she always insisted my work in Detroit was more important. So, I was continuously putting it off.

I tried to call Aunt June around July, I wanted

to visit her for my birthday but hadn't heard back from her as I usually did. I had already taken work off and was planning on buying the plane ticket but needed to be sure she would be home. Since I left, she picked up on her travels again though not as consistently as all those years ago.

I waited until the next day to try and reach out to her again when Katie called me.

It was a pleasant surprise considering I spoke to her just a few days before, she was in Carbondale visiting family before her senior year at ASU. "Hey Katie, how's it going back home?"

She didn't sound well. "Kenny, listen. I went to visit June this morning. She didn't come to door, so I let myself in. She was still in bed, but she wasn't breathing Kenny. I am so sorry. I called an ambulance, but it was too late."

My heart dropped to my stomach.

"Kenny, are you there?"

"I'm here." I couldn't speak. I needed to sit down but I couldn't move or wrap my mind around what I just heard. June and I spoke a week ago. I called her yesterday. I should have called again. I should have had someone check on her.

"You're her only family Kenny." Katie's voice was hoarse. It was clear she had been crying and she was right. I was the only family she had left. And she was mine.

I headed for the airport as soon as I got my mind clear enough through the fuzz. After a poorly attempted email sent to work explaining my impromptu absence, I was boarded on the plane and headed straight to her.

Chapter Twenty

Aunt June's funeral was beautiful. She never believed in traditional things such as caskets and grand halls. She went out just as she had wanted to. She was cremated, and a ceremony was held at her home. At least a hundred people attended, bringing with them flowers, liquor, and memories to share.

I always knew Aunt June was strange and well versed in the world, but I had no idea to what extent. From the stories her friends shared with laughter through the tears, June was notorious for her protests and humanitarian work across the globe. She led groups through DC, Standing Rock and the Wall on the Mexican border.

She moved to the UK one week, for no reason and with no explanation, later to have an on-again off-again relationship with Phil Collins. When she moved back stateside, she hiked the Appalachian Trail from Maine to Georgia in sixty days, rumor had it she went barefoot until Pennsylvania. Which I wouldn't believe if I hadn't met her. She moved to India during what most people at the memorial agreed was her midlife crisis. She went to join a missionary and lived with the monks for a short while taking a vow of silence. To no surprise to anyone, that vow didn't last.

Shortly after returning from India, June got serious about her Art. She moved to Seattle and started selling her work. She built a clientele quickly, with everything she had experienced in her life and her passion, her art was nearly as labored as breathing. While in Washington she met a man. He'd flown to Seattle on business from Denver, and he was completely taken by her. He extended his stay in Seattle for as long as he could, but when his time to leave arrived, he wanted her to go with him.

To those closest to her, it came as a complete shock she agreed. June was a free spirit and went where the times took her. Things were good for several months until the constraints of a serious relationship drove her out. She'd fallen in love with Colorado and wasn't ready to leave but was tired of him and the city. So she packed her bags, jumped in her Nova and hit the I-70 headed West. When a wrong turn landed her with an empty gas tank in Carbondale, she unpacked her bags and never left.

The town fell in love with her almost as quickly as she fell in love with it. She stayed at a motel off the route for a couple of weeks until the house we held this very memorial at had gone up for sale. She took it off the market before its first viewing.

And the rest was history.

By mid-day everyone was intoxicated, be it by the sadness, joy, or liquor. Tears came and went as did some people. Katie stood by me every step of the way. Samuel was in Alabama for a training program and couldn't leave without compromising his position that season. He was playing Varsity Quarter Back his Senior year and Aunt June would be livid if he threw it away.

Katie stayed after the memorial to help clean up, and we shared stories of our own. She was apparently extremely uncomfortable around June the first several times she had come around because June was such a hugger and always wanted to talk about Samuel. June placed a bet with herself that Katie and Samuel would be married one day and they both denied it. In no time, Katie came around and the two of them became close. They discussed her studies and dreams, June shared insight she gathered over her years. They always appeared so friendly with one another it never occurred to me that June may have been an acquired taste for anyone other than myself.

June's attorney and close friend I had met several times over the years came by the house the day before I was due back in Detroit. He was there to present her estate, being her only living family she left everything to me. He went over the fine print and explained the process to me. I assured him I didn't need a walkthrough, considering this wasn't the first time I had to endure this legal process. And I hoped I would never have to again.

I debated selling her property, but it seemed wrong, selling my parent's condo was difficult, but this was something different. I may have spent most of my life in Detroit, but I grew up in Carbondale. Aunt June's home is where I learned to drive, where I learned my art. It's where I made friends with Samuel and Katie. It's where I fell in love for the first time.

Aunt June's home was my home. It was the only home I ever really had.

Aware I couldn't maintain property in Carbondale and Detroit, I had to decide. I had enough money to live comfortably but not by stretching myself that thin. I mulled over my options. I couldn't abandon my dad's company, but I couldn't abandon June either. As I ruffled through my belongings left behind in my room, I found an envelope with my name on it written in Aunt June's silky cursive, delicately placed next to the copy of *The Shining* I left for her.

Wondering how it got there and what it was, I walked down the stairs to check if I was alone. I opened the envelope and sat down at the dining room table.

My Sweet Kenny,

If you're reading this, I must be gone.

I want you to know that I love you, more than anything in this world and the next. I was so angry with your mother when she left me to be with your father, but when they had you I realized I could never have room in my heart for anger while there was someone as beautiful as you on this earth to love.

When we first met, you were six years old and I went to see you and your mother in Michigan. I never forgot the time we spent together, you and your trains were a highlight of my life. There are some things I think are only fair for you to know.

That year, I was diagnosed with Lymphoma. Most people can live healthy lives after treatment, but I wasn't one of them. My treatments would work, and then they wouldn't. I went to see your mother and you in hopes of meeting you at least once in my life. I thought to myself, that the kindest thing I could do, was never see you again after that. I didn't want to risk getting close to you just for me to leave you behind one day. I thought I was making the right decision, but it is the biggest regret of my life.

When your parents passed, I knew you were coming to live with me and I was frightened I would wind up leaving you after all, despite the effort I put in to avoid such a thing in the first place. I went to my doctor, in hopes of better news. That maybe there was something they could do, but to no avail.

I am so sorry to of kept this from you for so long. It wasn't my intention. Every time I thought to tell you it just seemed best to let you be happy. I didn't want you being angry with me or yourself or this world. You came to me so broken and lonely, and you have blossomed into such a strong, kind and loving man. I didn't want to risk your growth, not with this. Not with something that wouldn't have changed, whether you knew about it or not.

Please don't be angry with me. You showed me what real love feels like, you gave me everything I had been chasing around the world all these years. You gave my life a purpose it never had before.

Our home is yours now. So are your cousins (You can't think it's weird for me to call the dogs your cousins anymore. You're not allowed).

You deserve to be happy Kenny, there is too much good in this world to let it go unnoticed. I've lived my life. Now it's time to live yours.

I love you dearly my Sweet Kenny,

June

I wanted so badly to be angry, despite her pleas not to be. She was sick all along. From the very beginning and I had no idea. She never let on, she was dying and made every day about me. I felt sick, the calloused hole in my heart burned, trying to rip through me again. My face wet from the tears I was too distraught to realize now soaked my chest.

Katie came running through the backdoor as I hit the floor screaming, wrapping her arms around me trying her best to console me while heartbroken herself. Aunt June had touched so many more lives than my own, and that made it harder. To know she was so good in this world but taken from it. Leaving all of us alone and lost without her. I wasn't angry with her; I was angry with myself.

The feeling of regret, that if I had known maybe I could have done something. If I'd known I would never have gone back to Detroit, I would have stayed here with her. I would have taken care of her, helped her. But I didn't.

I stayed sobbing on the floor for so long time was lost. Late the next morning I awoke still on the dining room floor, with a blanket over me and a tear-soaked pillow under my head. The last thing I remember was Katie holding me as I laid there, she must have waited there for hours the night before. As I sat up, I saw Katie laying on the floor opposite me, still asleep with a pillow and blanket of her own.

As I sat there and thought about what she had given up over the last week being there with me, I thought to thank Aunt June. If it wasn't for her making me have people over for my seventeenth birthday all those years ago, I never would have invited Katie and Samuel to our home. We may never have become friends, and I would really be alone in this world.

June always encouraged crying; I would never bite if I could avoid it. I was a grown man and could handle myself accordingly but there was something eye-opening and therapeutic about it that I had never appreciated until that moment. Everything had become so clear. My life in Carbondale has been the only place I ever truly felt at home and I knew what I needed to do.

Chapter Twenty-One

I woke Katie and asked her to join me on a morning hike. I would normally go alone, but this was a special occasion, and I couldn't forget my cousins. They had been rather lethargic since I got back, surely aware June was gone. They needed the trip as badly as I did.

I could recall one of the first conversations Aunt June and I ever had. She mentioned the Hot Springs, wanting me to join her and we never got around to it. She said she would spend eternity there if it was possible. So as my attempt to give my Aunt something even half as wonderful as she had given me over the years, Katie and I walked her ashes through the pines and to the Springs with the dogs in tow.

We reached a secluded area of the Springs and had a moment of appreciation for my Aunt once more. Before I spread her ashes into and around the waters, Katie stopped me and collected a small vial to be kept separate.

As we walked back to the house, there was

a familiar car in the drive, and Samuel was sitting on the hood.

It was relieving to see him, but I was worried about his training. We all caught up and Samuel explained his absence was excused due to a death in the family, he insisted June was every bit his Aunt as she was mine. He apologized for missing the memorial, but I couldn't let him feel down on himself. It gave me a proper excuse to recount the outlandish stories I heard a few days earlier during her 'Celebration of Life' as her will requested we call it.

I grabbed a bottle of June's good whiskey off the shelf and we sat around the dining room table, the dogs cuddled at our feet. Sharing stories about June and about our own successes and lives over the few years before, the afternoon turned to evening, the sunshine overthrown by starlight.

In the morning, over coffee and whiskey regrets, I made an announcement.

"I'm leaving today, to head back to Detroit. And I've decided while I'm there, I will be selling my house. And quitting my job." I felt a surge of pride move through me. I was never one for big changes, but for the first time in my life, I felt like I knew who I was and where I was meant to be. "If everything goes well, I should be back in a week. Katie, I know you have to head back to Arizona at the end of the month, but would you mind to staying here for a little while and watch over the dogs?"

Katie beamed with excitement "Absolutely!

It would be an honor. We are so excited for you." She grabbed Samuel's hand as he smiled at her.

They must have caught my confusion. I had seen them hug and be playful for years now, but something was different. "I'm sorry, 'We'? Are you speaking collectively, or did I miss something?" I already knew from the fear in their eyes as they both placed their hands on their laps. I couldn't help but laugh.

Samuel spoke first "I'm sorry man, we wanted to tell you, it's new. It's been a little off and on since Christmas, and we kind of just made it official when she came to see me before making her way here."

I was elated. Samuel and Katie being together made all the sense in the world. Aunt June was likely celebrating in the Springs right now to know she was right all those years ago. "I couldn't be happier you guys, are you kidding? I always kind of hoped it would work out that way." I couldn't stop smiling, it was the first bit of good news I had received in a week and it couldn't have been better. I gave them a hug and pledged my support.

The next day, I left Samuel and Katie to watch Aunt June's place and headed back home to Detroit. The first thing I did was call a realtor and set an appointment for that afternoon. Seeing that money wasn't the issue at hand, I priced my place just at value and let the realtor approve whatever offer she could get the quickest, selling just under market within a few days.

I called an emergency meeting with the board members of my dad's firm and explained the situation. They offered to buy me out of the business, but we came to an agreement for a silent partnership. I would still be involved, though minimally. If they needed me for any reason, I would be a quick call away, everything they needed from me could be handled remotely.

Selling would have given me money to live on until I figured things out in Carbondale, but the monthly income from the firm would be a better fit long term. And I still had most of my inheritance.

By the end of the same week I flew into Detroit, I flew out for the very last time.

Chapter
Twenty-Two

Katie and Samuel stayed with me until the last minute when I got back. My belongings were being delivered at some point over the weeks to follow, but it felt good living in the past for a moment. The same tapestries and figurines lined each room, the same cat, the same plants. It was as if Aunt June was there with me. Having my friends so close helped me adapt to her being gone.

After Katie headed back to ASU for her Senior year and Samuel back to the University of Alabama for his, I reacquainted myself with Carbondale. I was gone for three years, but nothing had changed. One of my canvas' still hung in the library right where I left it. As I stood staring at it, remembering the time I spent working on it with Aunt June by my side I heard a familiar voice behind me.

"Sorry sir, that piece belongs to the library and isn't for sale." The was a hint of flirtation in her tone. I turned around and came face to face with Alana. She was there, in Carbondale with me. I was rushed with excitement and swept her off the ground in my arms as she laughed.

We promised to keep in touch after graduation, and we did try. Somewhere along the lines we just fell out. She was busy in her world and I was busy with mine. She started dating a fashion editor in New York and that was the last I heard of her.

Still smiling ear to ear I took a good look at her. She had gotten even more beautiful with the years. "What are you doing here? I thought you were in New York?"

She laughed and tossed her head back as if to say good riddance to the thought. She finished her program and was offered an entry-level position at a magazine in New York but decided after a few months of working there, she hated it. Her passion was in designing and creating clothes, not showcasing other designers. She moved back home to get her feet on the ground while figuring out her next big move.

We went to dinner that night and picked up right where we left off three years prior as if nothing had changed. I even picked her up in Aunt Junes Nova, just like old times.

Alana had heard about Aunt June's passing and apologized for not going to the memorial. She wasn't the type well equipped with handling death but expressed her condolences. She was there with me at that moment and that's all that mattered.

We dated for six months before I proposed. Neither of us wanted a big wedding, in part because

Alana was going to design her own dress, and we agreed it would be the star of the evening. We were married in the fall in June's backyard, and all our closest friends attended.

Katie shared the news of her and Samuel's pregnancy, and of his being drafted for the Denver Broncos. She graduated top of her class from Arizona State and was opening her own practice in the spring after the baby was born. While the commute wasn't ideal for Samuel's practice and games, they thought it best to live in Carbondale near their parents, so they could help Katie with their son while Samuel was away for the season.

As I sat by the fire with Katie and Samuel, I watched my wife dance and pose for pictures with her friends and family. I thought back to how it all started, around this same fireplace several years before.

Alana came running for me, apologized in a not-so-apologetic tone and stole me away to the dance floor. As Samuel laughed, Katie took his hand and dragged him along too.

Chapter
Twenty-Three

As years passed, Alana opened her own Bridal Boutique in town and business was booming. Word got around about the wedding dress she had made for herself and requests were coming in from nearly a hundred miles away.

I went against everything I was taught by my dad and his financial company and decided to sell my art for a living. It started off rough, there were times when Alana's success was the only success in the household and caused a strain in our still-new marriage. But we made it through. I was offered a job designing a mural for the city, it picked up just enough web action to get my own work off the ground. Since then I've had dozens of jobs that have taken me out of town and hundreds of pieces sold through my online shop, not to mention the custom requests.

By our third wedding anniversary, Alana came to me with news of our pregnancy. Everything in life had been so full of love and happiness, I could never imagine it was possible to bring more. We set a doctor's appointment for that week and made plans for Katie and Samuel to join us for dinner at our home that weekend to tell them the good news.

At our appointment, we were met with even more surprise to find Alana was already in her second trimester. I was going to be a father to a beautiful, healthy baby girl. We had big changes to make at home baby proofing and setting up the nursery, and not much time to do it. We would spend every moment the following months making sure everything was perfect.

The Saturday evening after our appointment, Katie and Samuel arrived a quarter to seven o'clock with their son Jackson in tow. It had been difficult those days between to keep such a secret from our closest friends, but I didn't need to hold it much longer.

Alana's refusal in our dinner date wine toast raised the expected eyebrows.

Katie, shameless with her assumptions broke the momentary silence.

"Alana," Her eyes averting to myself as a sly grin began to spill across her face, naturally and infectiously bringing me to purse my lips in anticipation. "Are you pregnant?" Katie nearly threw her glass across the room in excitable demand for information as Samuel's jaw hit the floor. His eyes wide with suspicion.

Alana squeezed my hand and shouted with delight confirming the allegation. Our home erupted in clamoring and questions of when Jackson would meet his new friend. Among the chatter of nursery colors and Samuel's experiences of his first weeks home from the hospital with their son, Katie askcd if we had a name in mind yet. She wanted to be ready with baby blankets and caps personalized with our baby's name on everything for when we leave the hospital.

I glanced at Alana, tonight was about her and our daughter. I wanted to be sure she maintained the spotlight at every moment, so I held the floor open for her. She took my hand and lovingly cocked her head towards our friends, never breaking my eye contact.

I took the lead and relished at the moment as my eyes began to burn, fighting back tears with the help of a grateful smile. "Her name is June."

Thank you to my sponsors.
Without you and your generous donations
to this project, this would never
have been possible.

Mom, Alexis L., Anthony C., Kristina G.,
Jamie L., Jasmine C.,
Shelby W., Lindsey F., Jesse E.L.,
Madison H., Kathryn V.,
Callen D., Saray G., Sarah R.,
Kimberly C., Maryem T.,
The Ortega Family, Savannah H.,
Cathy W., Vicky L., Melissa B.

CPSIA information can be obtained
at www.ICGtesting.com
Printed in the USA
FSHW011831061120

9 780578 776941